13 —

Buzzy and the River Rats

Buzzy and the River Rats

Tales of a Catskill Mountain Boyhood

Book I: Buzzy Moves In

Written by

John Clarke Hoffman

Illustrated by Eric Hilgerdt

MERCURY PRESS

Spring Valley, New York

ISBN 0-929979-58-3

Printed and published in the USA by:

MERCURY PRESS
Fellowship Community
241 Hungry Hollow Road
Spring Valley NY 10977

Dedication

This book is dedicated to the students of the Green Meadow Waldorf School whose love of stories inspired *Buzzy and the River Rats*, and especially to David, Peter, Christopher and Teresa who were my first audience.

Author's Note

I am often asked if the Buzzy stories are true. I reply that the stories are a mixture of truth and Catskill Mountain inspiration. The excitement, the friendships, the fears, the romance, the spirit of adventure are as true as the day they were experienced. But, I confess to having taken considerable liberty with characters, locations and events for the sake of a good story. I hope the people of Delhi, both past and present, will forgive me.

* * *

My thanks to Kay Hoffman, David Sloan and Martha Masterson for their help in editing the Buzzy stories, to Eric Hilgerdt for the illustrations and to Michael Mendelsohn for the cover. Special thanks to Gerald Karnow, MD and Mercury Press who saw this book to completion.

Contents

Chapter 1 – BUZZY MOVES IN

The Woolerton House

IT WAS THE SUMMER I was going into eighth grade that Buzzy's family moved into the three-story yellow clapboard house across the street. A big van truck arrived one Saturday morning, drove right up on the lawn, and four men began unloading boxes and furniture. My friend, Amos Potter, and I were tossing a baseball in my front yard. We put down our gloves and headed across the street. The house had been vacant for almost a year. It had been occupied by an old retired couple, Sadie and Samuel Woolerton, who had died within a month of each other in the fall influenza epidemic. We were curious to see who was moving in.

Once across the street, we sat down in the thick green grass and leaned back on our hands to watch. Slowly but steadily the men hauled furniture through the front door. In went beds, dressers, chairs, tables, mirrors, lamps, desks, and an ancient Kelvinator refrigerator. One of the moving men was only about five feet tall. The others called him Patty. Whenever there was a big item like a sofa or overstuffed chair, Patty'd bend down and two other men would load it on his back. Then he'd carry it in with one of the other men holding the legs to keep it balanced. I was amazed that Patty didn't collapse into a heap, especially going up the stairs.

"Let's get Scuff," Amos suggested after we'd watched awhile.

"Okay," I said, giving a nod, "but he usually sleeps late on Saturdays. He's probably still in bed."

Scuff was Dennis O'Keefe. He lived in a neat white house with tall shuttered windows next to the Woolerton house. His family owned a pharmacy on the main street of town.

We walked across the lawn and up a set of gray stone steps to the front door. Amos gave three loud knocks. The

3

two of us looked through the panes of frosted glass to see if anyone was moving about.

"Hey!" a high-pitched voice yelled overhead. "Who's down there?"

Amos and I jumped to the sidewalk and looked up. Scuff was peering from an upstairs window.

"Come on down," I said. "Someone's moving into the old Woolerton house."

Scuff's bushy blond head popped out of the window dragging a white lace curtain with it. I could see he was still in his pajamas.

"Someone's moving in next door?"

"Yeah, Scuff, and they've got two gorgeous daughters, redheads, that want to meet you," Amos announced.

"Oh yeah!" Scuff's blue eyes focused down his long, thin nose in the direction of the Woolerton house, "how do they know me? Do you figure they saw me at the store?"

" 'How do they know me?' he says," Amos mocked under his breath.

Scuff continued to stare at the house next door. "They sure do have a lot of furniture," he muttered, "but I don't see any girls."

"Forget it, Scuff," Amos shook his head.

"Come on down," I said. "We haven't got all morning to wait around for you. There's going to be a baseball game at the campus field."

"I just woke up. I ain't even dressed yet," he replied.

"You're lazier than a pet raccoon, O'Keefe," Amos said looking disgusted. "You and Fats should start your own hibernation club—spend the summers in bed."

"Maybe I need a lot of sleep. Maybe I'm still growing," Scuff protested.

"Maybe you need a shot of my aunt Sadie's liver tonic. That'd get you out of bed," Amos laughed.

"See you later." I gave a wave. As Amos and I started back toward my house, an enormous red and white station wagon came speeding down Elm Street, turned sharply at the Woolerton house, bounced up over the curb, and roared up the driveway sending grass and gravel flying into the street. It screeched to a stop next to the moving van. The doors burst open and out spilled thirteen people, a dog, two cats, and a parrot in a bamboo cage. The cage bounced off the running board and started rolling down the driveway with the bird flapping and screaming like crazy. A dirty little boy in brown shorts ran after it. He caught the cage, but the parrot pecked at his fingers so he tossed the cage in the grass. The two cats took off for the nearest tree, and the dog, a black and white cocker spaniel, raced up and about the porch barking at the moving men.

I'd never seen such a big family on Elm Street. There were eight kids and five adults. They assembled in a tight little group on the front lawn as if they were going to have their picture taken and looked over the house. Then a short, skinny lady with a cigarette in her mouth and a baby under one arm began yelling out orders. Each time she spoke, her head seemed to disappear in a cloud of smoke. The little kids didn't listen but went tearing off around the house. There was one tot with his pants half down. Every time he'd start to run, he'd trip and fall. Only the two oldest children paid any attention. One was a girl I figured to be my sister's age and the other a boy about my age. Both had round, freckled faces, ruddy cheeks, and dirty blond hair. You could tell from a mile away they were brother and sister. The boy stood a good head shorter than me, but he looked compact and sturdy. I was tall and lanky. He had quick blue eyes, a mischievous smile and a sort of cocky air about him. His sister was of medium height and pretty. But she seemed quite serious. I figured that was because she had to chase all those little kids around.

After the skinny lady had stopped talking, they all went into the house—all except the oldest of the three men. I figured with his bald gray head and bushy whiskers he must be a grandfather. He disappeared into the van. There was some banging and crashing and out he came with a rocking chair which he dragged onto the porch. There he seated himself, lit up a pipe, and proceeded to survey the neighborhood like he'd lived there all his life.

"What an interesting bunch," Amos said, scratching his head.

"Yeah," I nodded, "I wonder if the boy's in our class? He looks pretty rugged—and fast."

"He'd better be," Amos grinned. "When the Truckers find out there's a new kid on Elm Street, they're going to chase him all over town."

"He doesn't look like he'll scare so easy," I said.

"Wait'll Scutter and Jake Bonner work him over, he'll be plenty scared," Amos replied.

"Yeah," I sighed, remembering that earlier in the summer Roy Scutter, Jake Bonner, and four other members of the uptown Trucker gang had caught Barney Shaw and me after a band concert. They pulled the grate off a storm drain and stuffed us head first into a pipe full of mud and wet leaves. I was plenty scared.

We watched the movers for a few more minutes, then crossed the street to my house. Shortly, Fats Lenahan and Mickey Harrington bicycled by yelling the game was starting at the campus. Amos and I grabbed our gloves and bats, jumped on our bikes, and followed them up Elm Street.

Late To School

With the leaves beginning to change and school approaching, I almost forgot about the new family across the street. I say "almost" because the little kids were all over the neighborhood chasing cats, climbing porches, and romping through flower beds. One morning Grandpa discovered the baby splashing merrily in our birdbath. We figured one of the older kids dropped him off for a quick dip. Another morning the smallest girl, Lena, got into our berry patch and ate herself sick on red currants. Mom had to administer bicarbonate of soda. But after a few weeks the neighbors got used to the kids being around, and Elm Street settled back to normal. Every once in a while I'd see the older boy and his sister, but with baseball, my regular lawns to mow, and Mom dragging me off to Oneonta for new school clothes, I never got over to meet them. The last days of summer vacation passed quickly. Before I knew it, I was eating breakfast and the school bell up on Sheldon Hill was tolling the five minute warning.

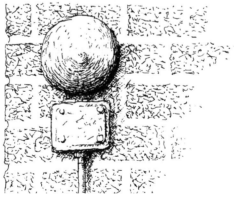

"Got to go," I muttered, pushing away a half-finished bowl of cereal. I just managed a kiss for my mom, grabbed my paper bag lunch, and tore out the back door.

"Finish your cereal from now on," Dad yelled after me. "There are people starving in this world!"

Down into the backyard I ran, past the barn, and through the orchard. At the fish pond, I cut across onto the Lackland estate and headed for the river. Normally I walked down Elm Street to the Kingston Street bridges to get to school, but when late I used the river path.

'Darn!' I thought to myself as I ran. 'I should have gotten up with my sisters. They left a half hour ago and are already sitting in their homerooms. They warned me.'

I had two sisters: Kaye, a year older and a freshman in high school, and Karen in the fourth grade.

'I'm going to be late the first day of school. And this year I've got Granny Gromley for homeroom teacher—the meanest, toughest, old battle-axe in the school. She's going to hate me all year for being late the first day. I'll probably miss opening assembly and everything, and get chewed out in front of the entire eighth grade. I'll have to spend the morning in Mr. Wiggins' office sitting straight up in a hard wooden chair staring at a blank wall.'

With the miserable vision of Miss Gromley chewing me out in front of the entire eighth grade and the morning spent staring at a blank wall, I hit the river path and started through the first of six backyards between the Lackland estate and the bridges. They were big, spacious yards with clumps of lilac and birch, and scattered flower beds. Usually I loved to wander among the beds watching the insects and enjoying the fragrance, but today I didn't see or smell anything—I was racing the school clock.

Mist from the river lay heavy along the bank. The butternut and willow seemed to be floating in a white sea. In and out of the thick clouds I ran, guided only by the memory of the hundreds of times I'd run the path before. Beyond the Sloan wood lot, the mist began to retreat and the yellow sun broke through. I'd covered five backyards in less than a minute and approached Miss

Panky's white picket fence. We usually avoided the Panky yard because she made such a fuss about her grass getting trampled. But today I was desperate. To go around would mean a loss of precious seconds. Without breaking stride, I vaulted the fence and dashed across the neat green lawn for the bridge walk.

"You! Young man! What are you doing on my lawn?" A thin, harsh voice screamed from the porch.

"Just my luck," I groaned, "Miss Panky had to be out sweeping."

"Stop! Stop I say! Come back here!"

I kept running.

"I know you! You're that Hoffman boy up the street! I'm going to call your mother right now! I'm going to tell her that her son is a trespasser!"

'Great,' I thought, 'now I'm in trouble with the neighbors. I'm a trespasser—whatever that is.'

I ran up a stone abutment, climbed over the safety rails, and started across the first of two bridges. Up on Sheldon Hill the final warning bell rang. I could never make the hill in one minute. I shuffled to a stop and looked around. There was no one else on the bridges or the Sheldon Hill path. A lone traffic guard stood at the intersection of Main and Kingston Streets. In another week, there'd be plenty of late stragglers for company— but not the first day of school. I gave a deep sigh, leaned over the bridge rail, and gazed down into the gentle rippling water. The mist had almost burned off. Silver fish darted among the rocks and shallow pools. A shaggy muskrat popped his head from under a muddy bank.

'I might just as well run away,' I thought to myself, 'maybe join the army or French Foreign Legion. That's what great Granddad did. He ran away and joined the Civil War when he was fourteen—just a year older than me. He didn't need any schooling. He got captured, escaped from a Confederate prison in Georgia, wrote a book, and became mayor of Malone—all without ever putting one foot inside an eighth grade.'

My stomach was beginning to ache. I didn't really feel like running away. The first day of school was almost as exciting as Halloween. There'd be all my friends to see, donuts for snack, and recess football. Besides, Christina Wetzel would be back from visiting relatives.

Christina was the local doctor's daughter. I'd been in love with her since the third grade. The Wetzels had come over from Europe and settled in Delhi after the war. Our church had sponsored them. I remember the first time we met was in the church meeting room. Christina was standing with her parents and the minister. She wore a white satin dress and black polished shoes. She had light brown eyes, pale delicate skin with a scattering of freckles around her nose, and dark red hair that fell to her waist. When the minister introduced us, Christina gave me a shy, warm smile. You could have knocked me over with a feather. After that fateful meeting, I was silently devoted to Christina. I tried to keep it secret, even from my friends, and if she liked me, she kept it secret too.

"Hey, John!" a voice yelled behind me. "Wake up, you bonehead!"

I spun around. There was Owen Blanchard with his uncle Anton in a dilapidated pickup truck. The radio was blasting a Hank Williams western tune and the truck seemed to be shaking in time with it.

"Jump in the back, quick, or we'll be late for school." Owen's head and arm were hanging out of the window. He motioned toward the back with his thumb.

We called Owen "Okie." He was a big, hillbilly kid with thick glasses and suspendered overalls. We were good friends, but I'd been told never to ride with his uncle Anton. Anton was regarded as a sort of madman around Delhi. He'd do anything for a bet. I once saw him drink a quart of beer while hanging by one arm off the creamery water tower. Up at his farm on Cobbs Cobble he had a confederate mortar which he fired off whenever he got moody, sending rocks and buckshot raining over the countryside. Nobody ventured on the property without carrying a white flag. I knew Anton was crazy all right, but how could I refuse a ride that might get me to school on time?

"Thanks," I said, climbing up on a low bridge beam and jumping for the truck bed.

Before I even hit, a cloud of black smoke belched from under the frame, the tires screamed, and the truck leapt forward. I landed in a heap, slid a couple of feet, and slammed into the tailgate with a bang. Anton gave me a big, wild grin in the rearview mirror. He had only three teeth in his upper jaw and his eyes seemed to be looking in different directions. Across the Kingston Street bridges we roared, then up Sheldon Drive. The truck rounded the stone wall entrance to Delaware Academy

11

and Central School on two wheels, raced through the faculty parking lot weaving among the cars, bounced over a curb, and sped up a 'pedestrians only' walkway.

"Holy cow!" I moaned, my head beginning to swim, "I should've stayed on the bridge. If I don't get killed, I'll end up in juvenile court for sure."

Out onto the wide green lawn in front of the school Anton drove, then straight toward the two-story, red brick building. I closed my eyes and held tight onto the tailgate. Suddenly, the truck swerved and lurched to a stop. I slowly opened my eyes and looked up. There, gazing out through the windows of the eighth grade homeroom, were the astonished faces of my classmates. The truck had stopped within an inch of the building.

Rusty Cooper threw open a window. "Hurry!" he shouted. "Miss Gromley's in the hallway!"

Okie opened the cab door and jumped up into the bed. Together we climbed through the open window and scrambled for two vacant seats. I was still clutching my lunch bag, which now looked like a crumpled sock. I threw open the desktop, chucked in the bag, slammed down the top, and sat with my hands folded.

The final bell rang. Miss Gromley strode stiffly into the classroom, her leather heels rapping the oak floor. She stopped in front of a small American flag that hung from the board and surveyed the room. My classmates and I sat straight and silent in our seats. Miss Gromley was only five feet tall, but her slate gray eyes had a look of cold steel. Even seniors like big Mike McShane cringed in her presence.

"Why is that window open?" Miss Gromley's beak-like nose thrust forward and her thin lips tightened.

No one spoke.

"Peggy Smith, close the window."

Peggy stood up and closed the window. Outside there was a sudden roar and Anton's truck sped out across the lawn. It crossed two concrete walks and disappeared down the granite steps in front of the main office.

My stomach went into a flurry of butterflies as I stared at Miss Gromley, wondering what horrible thing was going to happen next. But she didn't shriek or run out of the room or anything. She just turned to the class with a stern look and said, "That man should be in jail." I glanced over at Owen and could see he was biting his lip to keep back a grin.

Trouble On The Playground

After the pledge of allegiance and announcements over the public address system, the eighth grade filed down to the auditorium for opening assembly. There were twenty-eight of us in the class: nine girls and nineteen boys. We sat in the balcony with the seventh grade. Downstairs was reserved for the high school.

I sat between Amos Potter and Mickey Harrington. They were two of my best friends. Amos was a stocky kid of medium height with dark brown hair, dark eyes and skin, and a square, angular face. His father was English and his mother a mixture of Dutch and Iroquois Indian. The family ran a small dry cleaning business on upper Main Street. Amos was about the fastest runner in the school. The high school track coach even let him train with the track team, which was a great honor. He attributed his great speed to the fact that he lived at the foot of Meredith Street and had grown up running to keep from getting beaten up by the tough, uptown Trucker gang. Amos was also about the quietest kid in our class. He hardly ever spoke, and when he did, it was usually about hockey or baseball. He loved sports and couldn't wait to grow up and play on a "pro" team.

13

Mickey Harrington was about the same size as Amos, but wiry and rough. He sometimes gave me a feeling of being all elbows. He had intense blue eyes, a short bumpy nose, and reddish brown hair which he kept in a short crewcut. "Mick", as we called him, was a leader in the class—not because he was popular, but because he was pushy and got things done. He loved sports too and fancied himself a great boxer. In his spare time, he built model ships and airplanes out of balsa wood. He had a real genius for that. Most of us bought kits, but Mickey made his own designs and cut the pieces. Sometimes he'd donate one of his planes for a "terminal" flight. We'd stuff it with firecrackers, wind the propeller until the rubber band was ready to break, set fire to the wings, and chuck it off the cliffs above Steele Creek. Down she'd go in a cloud of flames and explosions, just like in the movies. Mickey's father was minister of the First Presbyterian Church on Clinton Street.

Sitting next to Mickey was Dennis O'Keefe. Dennis was my neighbor and long-time friend across the street. He stood a couple of inches shorter than me, was skinny, and what we called a "towhead". That meant he had hair so blond it was almost white. He wore it in a "flat-top" or crewcut that was flat on top. O'Keefe was mostly Irish, quick-tempered and pesky. I guess that's why we called him "Scuff". He was always pulling pranks and could rile me quicker than anyone. Once in the seventh grade, he tied one end of a fishing line to Cathy Stewart's notebook and a fishhook to the other end. As I was going up to the board to do a math problem, he hooked my pocket. I pulled all Cathy's books onto the floor. It made a terrible racket. The teacher thought I'd knocked the books off on purpose and made me stand in a corner for the morning. After school, I chased Scuff all the way home. He was lucky I didn't catch him. It had just rained and I was

14

planning to stuff him into the nearest mud puddle. That's what we called making a "chocolate bar."

Next to Scuff sat Franklin "Fats" Lenahan, another good friend. Fats was short and plump. He had fuzzy brown hair, a round angelic face, and calm blue eyes. His family ran the town's only appliance store. Everyone liked Fats but some of the boys made fun of him. Barney Shaw was the worst. He'd do things like tape "KICK ME" signs to Fat's back, steal his lunch and hang it from the top of the swings, glue his desk shut, and stick cocklebur in his gym shorts. But Fats was no wimp. Once he got mad, we all kept out of his way, even Barney Shaw.

Barney "Weed" Shaw usually sat with us at assemblies, but he'd been snagged out of line for clowning and was sitting in the middle of the girls. Weed and I had been friends since kindergarten. He stood about my height, had wavy black hair, dark brown eyes and a large handsome face that always seemed to be smiling. Weed was a great guy but always in trouble. You never knew what crazy thing he'd do next. He might chuck your books out the window or bean you with an eraser while a teacher stood two feet away. By eighth grade he'd already been suspended twice: once for letting a rat loose in the library, and once for causing a minor panic in the girls' bathroom by yelling "fire drill" during class recess. He was on what the school board called "permanent probation". Weed, Fats, Amos, Scuff, Mickey, Okie, three other boys and I were the class "townies." The rest of the boys and all but three of the girls lived on outlying farms.

"Shhh! Shhh!" Miss Gromley came creeping down the balcony aisle. "Mr. Wiggins is about to speak."

Two seventh grade boys were talking to each other and didn't hear her. She reached over, caught one of them by the ear and twisted it until he was practically standing in his seat, both cheeks glowing red with embarrassment.

We all started to snicker, but she froze us quick with one of her icy glances.

Mr. Wiggins came out from behind the stage curtain, looked about the auditorium, and cleared his throat. He was a large, portly man with thick black hair, an enormous nose, and a trim little mustache.

"Welcome to the 1954-55 school year at Delaware Academy and Central School. I trust you all had a refreshing and renewing summer and, like me, are looking forward to an industrious school year. On this first day I want each of you to ask yourself, 'What new goals can I set for myself at Delaware Academy?'"

It was sounding pretty much like last year's opening speech. Mickey, Amos, and I slumped down and pressed our knees into the seat backs in front of us. Amos nodded a couple of times, closed his eyes, and dozed off. Mickey reached into his pocket and pulled out a ping-pong ball. We took turns making a hoop with our thumb and forefinger while the other took shots at it by squeezing the ball out of his fist. It was a risky game, but that's what made it fun.

Mr. Wiggins' speech was short. He was renowned for short speeches. Everyone applauded. Mr. van Arns, the assistant principal, stood up, introduced three new teachers, and read a list of school rules. Then Daniel Page, a senior, recited a poem about the Greek gods. According to the poem, the gods spent most of their time stealing each other's wives and plotting revenge. The poor Greek peasants ended up getting the worst of it. Daniel was followed by four high school girls playing their flutes. They played longer than the speech, poem, and announcements put together. Mickey got careless during one piece and shot the ping-pong ball between the seats in front of us. It bounced off the armrest and dropped over the balcony rail. There was a big stir below. I held my breath expecting any second to be yanked out of my seat. Miss Gromley walked down to the balcony rail and scratched her head. Then Mr. Becker, the high school drafting teacher, burst through the balcony doors holding the ping-pong ball like it was a poison dart or maybe radioactive. He hurried down the aisle and showed it to Miss Gromley. With grim faces they began eying the rows for suspects. Most of the students shrugged or shook their heads. A couple pointed at the seventh graders. When their eyes fell on Mickey and me, we stared straight ahead as if we were totally absorbed in the flute music. Inside we felt like scrambled eggs. Finally they gave up and Mr. Becker went back downstairs. Miss Gromley must have concluded it was seventh graders because she gave them a long stern look before sitting down.

At the end of the assembly we stood and sang the school alma mater, then filed back to the classroom. The rest of the morning was fun. Miss Gromley gave us a whole hour of recess, and Mickey, Barney, and I got to cart textbooks around the school until noon. At noon we went out onto the playground for lunch. The ninth and tenth grades were out with us.

A group of us had just finished playing football and were sitting on a grassy knoll eating our lunches when Amos nudged me and said, "Look over by the tennis courts...the Truckers are up to something."

I glanced over and saw Roy Scutter and his brother Luke leaning against the chain link fence. Roy was tall and lean, his sandy hair combed straight back with a high wave in front. He had pale yellow eyes. A sly smirk played across his freckled face. Luke stood a head taller and outweighed his brother by a good thirty pounds. He had a low forehead, thick nose and large square jaw. Straggly blond hair hung over his face and ears. Surrounding Roy and Luke were most of the members of the Meredith Street Trucker Gang. Roy was the leader. They were laughing and looking in the direction of the jungle gym. I turned toward the jungle gym and saw the new kid from across the street sitting on a low rung eating a sandwich.

"They're going to do something to that new kid," Scuff spoke in almost a whisper.

"Maybe we should warn him, or invite him over," Amos said.

Fats sat up in alarm. "Forget it," he glared at Amos. "We've got enough trouble with the Truckers. I say my prayers every time I get home safe from school. Don't be sticking your nose in."

"I'm with Fats," Scuff nodded. "Let the new kid find out about the Truckers the hard way."

"I say we stick our noses in," Weed spoke up. "I ain't scared of those guys."

"You should be," Fats scoffed, "they've kicked you around plenty. Maybe you think they've been playing games."

"Yeah, Weed, I heard Luke and Billy Bones dropped you into the septic pit at the fairgrounds last month," Ben Laney spoke up. Ben was a short, skinny kid with a big head, buck teeth, and a great mop of light brown hair. He was the smartest kid in the class. We called him "Tweets" because he sometimes whistled when he talked.

"They tried, but I put up a fight. I only got my socks and sneakers wet," Weed shrugged. "Mom made me bury the sneakers," he added with a laugh.

"What do you two say?" Amos turned to Mickey and me. Mickey had been resting in the grass. He sat up and looked around. "The Truckers won't risk a fight on the playground. Isn't that right, John?"

"Don't know," I said. "Let's see what happens. If they gang up on him, we'll help."

"If they gang up on him, you can help," Fats muttered. "Count me out."

"Count me out too," Scuff said. "We haven't even got Okie out here to help us."

"Look," Mickey interrupted. "Something's going to happen."

A big, pudgy kid with dark greased hair, a stubby nose and tiny black eyes broke from the group and started for the jungle gym. He wore a black leather jacket with a skull and crossbones on the back. A heavy chain hung in a loop from his belt. It was Turk McGraw, the worst bully in the school, and "enforcer" for the Truckers. He swaggered over to the jungle gym, stopping a few feet from the new kid.

"Give me your sandwich," he sneered, sticking out his hand.

The new kid looked up but kept eating. Turk grabbed him by the hair and reached for the sandwich. A fist suddenly shot through the air and there was a loud splat. McGraw howled and staggered back, covering his face. Blood was trickling through his fingers. He made so much noise that Claude Perkins, one of the custodians, came running out of the shop behind the tennis courts.

"What happened here?" he demanded as he ran up.

Roy and a couple of the gang members had already come over and were standing next to Turk.

"Uh...he fell and hit his nose on the jungle gym," Roy spoke.

Claude looked suspiciously at the three boys. "Is that the truth?"

"Yeah," Jake Bonner, a weasely kid with a front tooth missing and a thick scar along his right jaw, stepped forward. "He was climbing and slipped."

Claude looked at the third boy, Gideon Spickey. Gideon stood only about five feet tall but he was solid muscle. His head was shaved and he had a tiny red dagger tattooed on one arm."Dangerous piece of equipment," Gideon replied with a smirk.

Then Claude turned to the new kid who was still sitting on the jungle gym eating his sandwich. "What do you have to say about this?" he asked.

The new kid looked up. "He got hurt on the jungle gym," he answered. "He's real clumsy."

Seeing he was getting nowhere, Claude finally said, "Take him to the nurse's office. His nose may be broken."

Roy and Jake took Turk by the arms and the three of them headed across the playground for the rear entrance. The rest of the Truckers scattered toward the bus garage. The new kid was still sitting on the jungle gym eating his sandwich.

"Wow! Did you see that?" Scuff burst out excitedly. "He pasted McGraw right in the nose!"

"And hard too," Amos agreed.

"I didn't even see his fist move it was so fast," Mickey chuckled.

"Yeah, just the beautiful sound of Turk's nose crumpling into his ugly puss," Fats beamed.

"He shouldn't have hit McGraw," Tweets broke in.

"What are you talking about, Tweets?" Weed roared. "McGraw was asking for it. Maybe you think he should have just handed over his lunch and maybe kissed McGraw's hand."

"That isn't what I'm saying," Tweets shot back. "I'm saying he shouldn't have hit Turk, because now the Truckers are going to be laying for him, and sooner or later they're going to get him, and it isn't going to be funny."

"Tweets is right," Amos nodded, "they'll get the new kid. They're good at that."

"Yeah, you're probably right," Scuff sighed, "but like Fats said, it sure did sound nice."

The bell rang ending lunch period. We gulped down the rest of our lunches and hurried for the double doors at the rear of the building. As we crowded through, I felt a sharp poke in my ribs. Next to me stood big Luke Scutter.

"Saw you guys laughing at Turk out there," he said, leaning close. "Have to teach you kiddies some manners."

With that he grabbed me by the shirt and pants and threw me down the hall. If I hadn't run into a group of my classmates, I'd have gone sprawling on my face.

Christina Wetzel

The afternoon went almost as quickly as the morning. We got our lockers and played soccer in gym, learned about the town founder, Ebenezer Foote, in history class, and ended the day with a half hour of drill on percentage problems. Before Miss Gromley took final attendance, I left the classroom to get a drink at the fountain.

When I returned, there was Christina Wetzel standing by the door talking with her best friends, Fay Bibbins, Bunny Reimes, and Becky Chambers. It was the first time I had seen her since school ended in June. In the excitement of the day, I'd forgotten how all summer I'd looked forward to Christina returning from Europe. Now she was back and even prettier than before. She seemed older and more serious, but as she spoke, her brown eyes sparkled and her face filled with excitement.

I took a deep breath and sighed. She had hardly paid any attention to me last year. It was almost as bad having her back as it was having her gone.

"Hey, John," Scuff bumped me from behind. "What are you staring at?"

"Just thinking," I replied.

"Thinking about Christina Wetzel?"

"Don't push it, Scuff!"

"Can I help it if you've been chasing her since the third grade?" he laughed.

I clenched my fists. "You say another word and I swear I'll smash you," I muttered.

"Ooooow!" Scuff howled with delight as he danced behind me. He licked his finger, touched my shoulder, and made a hissing sound like steam.

I decided to ignore him and started for the classroom. As I walked through the door, Christina stopped talking, looked right at me, and smiled. It was like standing in the noonday sun. I opened my mouth to say "hi" but nothing came out. I felt my face redden. After a few seconds of feeling like an idiot, I managed to shut my mouth, smile back, and stumble into the classroom. Head hanging, I shuffled back toward my desk. Scuff was still behind me.

"Nicely handled, John," he said, slapping me on the back.

I turned and shot him a furious glance.

"Look, old pal," he continued, "next time Christina smiles at you, just try and get your mouth to go up and down, and I'll speak the words—like a ventriloquist and his dummy."

I swung around and grabbed for him. Scuff was quick, but I managed to catch his shirt. He tried to twist away but slipped and fell into a desk. The desk toppled with a crash.

"John Hoffman!" Miss Gromley's voice rang out from the front of the room. The whole class stared in horror. "Release Dennis and pick up that desk! After school tonight, you will sweep the entire room and arrange all the desks. Tomorrow you will forfeit lunch recess."

"Yes ma'am," I said, lifting the desk off the floor.

"Sorry," Scuff whispered, helping me. "I'd give you a hand after school, but I've got to work at the store. I'll keep you company at recess tomorrow."

I sat down in my seat. Fay Bibbins looked over at me with a silly grin and giggled. 'What a day,' I thought to myself, 'what a day!'

Fight At Gundy's Barn

The dismissal bell rang and my classmates hurried for the door. Within seconds, the room was empty except for Miss Gromley and me. I got up and began carefully arranging the desks in the first row.

"The broom and dust pan are in the closet," Miss Gromley said, getting up from her desk. "Close the door when you leave, and no more horsing in the classroom! Is that clear?"

"Yes ma'am," I replied contritely.

She stopped at the door to give me one last severe look and left the room.

I ran to the closet, grabbed the broom, and started racing in a snake-like pattern up one row and down another. If I saw a crooked desk, I gave it a good kick with my foot. After coming down the last row, I pushed the pile of dirt and paper under a radiator, threw the broom in the closet, and ran out of the classroom, completely forgetting about closing the door.

Outside it was warm and sunny. The air felt so fresh and alive after the dark corridors of the school that I paused for a moment and took a deep breath. From in front of the school on Sheldon Hill, I could see the length and breadth of Delhi. To the left spread the railroad yard with its rows of tracks, feed mills, creameries, and factories; in the center were the many streets, houses, stores, and churches of the village; and to the right lay the red brick county buildings and a scattering of farms stretching up the valley toward Stamford. There were so many trees that, except for a few three-story buildings along Main Street and a scattering of church spires, it was hard to tell a village existed at all beyond the railroad yard.

Across the valley on a broad plateau, tucked between Sherwood Mountain and Bell Hill, stood the white clapboard buildings and large dairy barn of the state technical college. It was referred to as Delhi Tech. Dad had taught history at the college and was now dean of students. Barney Shaw's father worked at the dairy barn. I could see the roof of their house just below the barnyard.

East of the college rose a huge, treeless hill broken into long rectangular fields of corn, barley, and hay. The hay shimmered golden in the sunlight, ripe for a second cutting. We called the hill "Bald Sadie." On top of the hill sat an ancient hay shed built of hand-hewn timbers. In summer we sometimes slept overnight in the shed. Underneath the floorboards was a hidden tunnel. Mickey and I had discovered it while playing hide-and-seek. It was about twenty feet long and two feet square. We figured the shed had once housed settlers and the tunnel dug to protect the children during Indian raids.

Bald Sadie stretched on over to Meredith Street, which is part of Route 28. Meredith Street was home to the Trucker Gang. They had their headquarters in Stutz's junkyard—the biggest junkyard in Delaware County. Through the trees I could just make out a yard crane and high ridge littered with wrecked cars. My greatest hope was to someday explore Stutz's. Whenever we drove to Oneonta, we passed the high board fence and dingy, tar-papered sheds of the yard. I'd been told that everything that had been built in the whole United States since the Civil War was stored away in those sheds. But with the Truckers sitting on top of the place, there seemed little hope of ever seeing anything but the board fence.

Beyond Meredith Street sprawled the twenty or so acres of Woodland Cemetery, and beyond the cemetery smoldered the fires of the town dump. The smoke stank something fierce. There were rats too—plenty of them. One night Mickey, Fats, Weed, and I snuck up to the dump with flashlights and BB guns. We'd heard about the rats and were going to see if we could shoot a few. We didn't turn on the flashlights until we got right to where the trucks dumped over a steep bank. Then at a signal we turned them on all at once. It was the eeriest sight I've ever seen. Thousands of tiny red eyes glowed back at us along the bank. It was like looking at the Milky Way on a summer's night, but alive and scary. A wave of squeals broke over the dump and rats began running in every direction, kicking over cans and bottles, and sliding about in the garbage. Some ran right at us. I could feel them scurrying past my legs. One bumped into Fat's sneaker and they both jumped about a foot in the air. We got out of there fast without firing so much as one BB.

Beyond the dump, the land dropped through pastures and wood lots to the valley. I looked up Route 10 toward Stamford, then across the flats to the river. The west branch of the Delaware River flowed dark and silent as it rounded the American Legion field and headed under the Bridge Street span into town. Just past the span, it entered the stone channel along Delaware Avenue, split in two behind Salter's Lumber Mill, and spilled through the rapids at the Kingston Street bridges. Below the bridges, it passed my backyard on its way to the Steele Creek rapids.

The river was my second home. I built and sailed my first raft when I was seven. My friends and I had explored every inch of the west branch from Bloomville to Delancy. We even had a secret camp on an island behind the Co-op Creamery. The Meredith Street Truckers were bullies of the town, but we were masters of the river.

"John, aren't you supposed to be at Mr. McCaffery's?" a voice called behind me. It was my sister Kaye. She had just come out of the school with her latest boyfriend, Wally Tibbs. Wally was balancing a pile of books with a violin case on top. Good old sister Kaye. She managed a new coolie for every season, and Wally Tibbs was a junior with his own car—a real catch for a freshman.

"Yeah, Sis, supposed to mow his lawn," I replied.

"Want a ride?" Wally asked, peeking over the violin case through his horn-rimmed glasses.

I'd had enough riding for one day and shook my head. "Thanks. I'll walk. Got to get in shape for basketball."

As they turned toward the parking lot, I took off at a run down a grassy hill into the woods. There was a blacktop walkway up Sheldon Hill, with concrete steps at both ends, but my friends and I preferred the pathways through the woods. It was good to know the paths in case you got chased by the Truckers.

All the paths ended at a small bicycle shed at the foot of Sheldon Drive. I skirted the shed, crossed Sheldon Drive, and continued on the sidewalk along the Andes Road toward the bridges. There were a few high school students on the sidewalk and some children trying to catch grasshoppers in the weeds. When I got to the bridges, I slowed my pace and gazed down through the metal rails at the swirling water below. It had rained the previous two days. The river was running swift and deep, great foamy swells lifting over the hidden rocks of the rapids. Weed, Scuff, and I were planning to raft downstream on the weekend to explore an old deserted mill, but the water looked dangerous. We might have to put it off for a week.

The first bridge ended on a narrow island half covered by a large factory building. As I passed the building, I began to hear shouts coming from behind Gundy's barn, just beyond the second bridge. I dashed across the second bridge and headed for the barn. Once there, I slowed and cautiously made my way along one side to the back. The shouts grew louder. I looked around the corner. At first all I could see was Turk McGraw, Roy Scutter, and Jake Bonner huddled around something on the ground.

I couldn't figure the Truckers fighting among themselves unless they were bickering over something they'd stolen. Bertie Grimes, another Trucker, stood a few feet to the side, laughing and chewing on a candy bar. Then in the dust I saw the new kid from across the street. Turk and Jake had him pinned to the ground, but he was swinging furiously with one free arm.

"I'll teach you to mess with me," Turk shouted as he grabbed for the free arm.

"Get off, you fat, stinking toad!" the kid yelled.

Roy took him by the hair and stuffed a handful of dirt in his face. Turk caught the free arm as Jake drove a fist into his stomach. The kid coughed and spat out the dirt. The next thing I knew, I was running full speed at the four of them. Bertie was so surprised he dropped his candy bar. I dove at Turk and Jake and hit them hard enough to send both on their backs in the gravel. Roy grabbed me around the neck, but the new kid punched him in the jaw. As Roy fell back, I slipped under his arm. Bertie tried to kick us from behind, but the new kid caught his foot and sent him sprawling on his face. The two of us scrambled to our feet and ran for the road. Roy, Turk, Jake, and Bertie sat dazed for a couple of seconds, then jumped to their feet and took off after us.

"Follow me," I said. "We'll shake them at Tillet's barn."

We crossed Kingston Street and raced down the middle of Elm. The Truckers were about thirty feet behind us. After the Tillet house, I cut into a cinder driveway and headed for a tall, wooden barn. The new kid was fast and staying right with me. Together we ran up to the big double door. It was only open a few inches and would hardly budge. The new kid just squeezed by. I quickly followed and had almost made it when Jake grabbed me by the shirt as he slammed into the door. He caught my pocket and tore it clean off. I pushed as hard as I could and managed to get through.

Inside it was dark, but that didn't bother me. I knew the place by heart. "This way," I said, working my way through a collection of lawn mowers and garden tools to a staircase. Up the stairs we ran, past an old workbench cluttered with them tools, and into a back room filled with furniture. Downstairs I could hear the four Truckers banging into the lawn mowers and knocking over rakes.

"Help me move this thing," I said, taking the arm of an old horsehair couch. Together we pulled the couch away from the wall. Behind it was a small door. I tripped the latch and the door swung open to the outside. The Truckers were now on the stairs. The two of us crouched in the opening and jumped. We landed in an alley between two barns. Behind the barns ran a thick juniper hedge.

"Which way?" the new kid asked.

"Out back," I said. "I know a way through the hedge."

Just then, a head popped around the front corner of the barn. It was Bertie.

"They're out here, Roy! They're out here!" he yelled.

I picked up a rock and threw it at him. He quickly dove for cover.

"Come on," I said. We raced through the alley and around the back of Tillet's barn. Near a birdhouse stuck on a post I dropped to my hands and knees and pushed aside the branches to reveal a narrow opening.

"Weed and I cut this hole last year," I said, crawling in. "I figured it'd come in handy."

The new kid followed. Together we passed through a dark tunnel of twisted limbs and sweet scented needles, and emerged on the other side in an apple orchard. Trees heavy with fruit stretched as far as the river. Bees hummed about the clover and wild flowers.

"We'll take the river path to the tree house," I said snapping off a bright red apple.

The new kid nodded and broke off an apple for himself. Down through the orchard we ran. Beyond the last row of trees, we picked up the river path. I glanced over my shoulder and saw the Truckers were nowhere in sight. We'd lost them at the hedge.

The Old Lackland House

"This is the Davis' backyard," I said, slowing the pace. "Old Mr. Davis is retired from the county. He used to give my sister Kaye and me rides on the steam roller when they were patching the roads."

We looked across a wide expanse of grass and clumps of birch trees and flower beds. Within a circle of trellised roses stood a marble statue of a Greek maiden, water pouring from a jar she held on her shoulder.

"The next place is the Lackland estate. They're our neighbors. Our house used to belong to the Lackland family—back when they still had big farms in town. They used it for the servants and hired hands. Now the family is gone. The daughter died when we were kids. My sister and I watched the funeral from Grandma's bedroom window. There was a horse-drawn hearse and everyone was dressed in black. Poor Mr. and Mrs. Lackland—they were really sad. She was their only child. Then Mr. Lackland died and Mrs. Lackland got dotty. She couldn't even get the car out of the driveway. She used to bang into the house and barn and trees. The car looked like it'd been in a demolition derby. They finally had to take her away. Now the place is deserted. The house and barn are great places to explore, and you can hide for days in the backyard. But you have to be careful because the police keep a sharp eye on the place. The house is full of valuable antiques."

We passed behind a large, unkempt yard where everything was green and in rampant growth. The bushes and trees were so thick they almost concealed the distant barn and house. Toward the rear of the backyard rose a strange mound of vines and thorny brush.

"What's that mound?" the new kid asked.

"There's an old brick garden shed hidden under there," I replied. "See that big jay sitting on the sumac branch? The peak of the roof is about a foot behind him. You have to crawl through to get to it. Plenty of snakes in there. Spooky too. Old Andy Burr who fishes the river at night says he's seen ghosts floating around the place. But the house is even spookier. I once got the life scared out of me in there."

The new kid gazed up toward the house. His face brightened with curiosity. "What happened? How'd you get the life scared out of you?"

31

Both of us stopped. I hooked my thumbs into my pants pockets and faced the new kid.

"First, you have to promise never to tell a soul, because we could get in big trouble. You promise?"

"Promise."

"Swear on your eyes?"

"Swear."

"Well, a few years ago, after they took Mrs. Lackland away, the two boys that live next to you—Brian and Dennis O'Keefe, my sister Kaye, her best friend Amy Lynn, and I got into the house. It was all locked up, but we got in through a cellar window. The window was hidden under the front porch and left ajar. Scuff, that's what we call Dennis, and I crawled under the porch trying to catch a stray cat and saw the window. Scuff told his brother, and I told my sister. One rainy Saturday afternoon we were all sitting around the house with nothing to do, so we decided to go over and explore the place. The five of us crawled under the porch and gathered around the window. I pushed it open and stuck my head in. Down below was an old root cellar with a dirt floor. Around the sides were racks for canning jars and wooden bins. The racks still had jars of pickles and peaches on them. One by one we crawled through the window and climbed down the rack, trying hard not to knock bottles off. Inside it was dark and dingy and smelled like a cave. After stumbling around for a while, we found a door that opened into a hallway. The hallway led to a staircase. Single file we climbed the stairs and found ourselves in a kitchen at the rear of the house. There was a small table in the kitchen set with plates and silverware, just like someone was getting ready to eat— except the plates were all dusty. The wall toward the front of the house had a doorway and a pass-through with a sliding door. When I tried the door in the doorway, I found it locked, which seemed kind of strange. Kaye and Amy started getting all scared and wanting to go home, but we told them it was probably locked by accident and not to worry. Once they settled down, we opened the sliding door in the pass-through. It connected the kitchen to a large dining room. In the dining room stood a huge table surrounded by twelve high-back chairs. The room walls were covered with gold print wallpaper and green silk drapes. The ceiling must have been twelve feet high. It was arched and had gold trim all around it. Glass chandeliers hung at either end. I'd never seen such a fancy place. But everything seemed old and musty—like nobody'd used the room for a long time. Everything except for a flower vase in the middle of the table. The flowers were wilted yet there was still something fresh about them. That was kind of spooky."

I stopped my story for a moment and looked around. I didn't want Roy Scutter and his friends sneaking up on us.

"Go ahead, finish the story," the new kid urged. "I'll keep an eye on the path."

"Well, Scuff and Brian and I wanted to climb through the pass-through, but the girls refused. They were still scared. We couldn't leave them alone in the kitchen, so instead we started poking around the cupboards. Then Brian opened a door and discovered a narrow staircase going upstairs. After a lot of convincing, Kaye and Amy agreed to go upstairs with us—but only if one of us went up first to make sure it was safe. Scuff and I said we'd go first and scout around. Up the stairs we climbed, changed direction on a landing about halfway, and continued to the top. At the top was another locked door, but this one had a key in it. I unlocked the door and let it swing open. Beyond was a wide hallway with doors on either side. 'Must be bedrooms,' I said to Scuff. We each took a side of the hallway and began checking the rooms. All the doors had been left open. Inside were bedrooms all right, each as fancy as the dining room. Some even had their own bathrooms. But one bedroom near the end of the hall was the fanciest. It was a little girl's bedroom with a canopied bed and piles of pillows and stuffed animals. The walls were covered in flowers and the ceiling painted with stars and a crescent moon over the bed, and a bright sun and clouds over the rest. One whole wall was lined with dolls, each one dressed in a different costume from places like Switzerland or Mexico or China. And in the middle of the room was the biggest doll house you've ever seen. You could crawl right into it. It had a bathtub, sinks, electricity— everything. We were so excited, we ran all the way back downstairs to tell the others. Kaye and Amy didn't believe us. They said we were making it up. We practically had to drag them up to the room. They took one look and almost fainted in the doorway. Then they ran in and started playing around. Brian and Scuff and I got tired of looking at the dolls and stuff pretty quick and left. At the end of the hallway was the main staircase and we wanted to explore the downstairs."

"Hold it! Someone's coming on the path!" the new kid interrupted.

We ducked into the brush. I hadn't heard a thing and wondered if he was bluffing. Shortly two children came along carrying lunch pails. They turned off behind one of the houses.

"You sure have good ears," I said.

The new kid grinned and we stepped back out onto the path.

"Did you get to explore the downstairs?" he asked.

"Yeah, Brian, Scuff, and I went downstairs. The staircase widened at the bottom and ended in a big hall. Straight ahead was the main entrance. To the right and left were pairs of large glass doors. One pair opened into a living room filled with old furniture, the other into an office. The office doors were partway open, so we decided to look in there first. We stuck our heads in and what a mess! Newspapers, books, magazines, and boxes were everywhere. A big desk with a typewriter and lamp on top was practically buried in papers. In one corner stood an ancient red and silver motorcycle, and above it hung a moose head with glass eyes. The walls were covered with portraits, photographs, hats, medals, autographed base-ball bats, and everything else you can think of. One photograph showed Mr. Lackland in college. Another showed him seated in a World War I biplane. We crept in for a closer look. I was especially interested in the photographs. But it seemed kind of spooky—almost as if Mr. Lackland was still around.

"We'd only been in the office a couple of minutes when the girls came running down the stairs. They saw us in the office and hurried to join us. They both looked pale. Kaye whispered excitedly that they didn't know where we'd gone, so they'd started back to the kitchen. On the stairs, they'd heard noises down below—shuffling and strange voices. She was sure there was someone in the house with us.

"Scuff, Brian, and I listened hard. At first, all I could hear was the rain tapping against the windows. But suddenly there were soft footsteps in the hallway—footsteps moving quickly towards us from the back of the house. We were so scared none of us could move. My body felt like a great dead tree and I was peering out through two knotholes. Scuff and Brian were trembling all over. Kaye and Amy were clutched together with their eyes closed. Then around the glass door came a tiny lady in an old fashioned dress and a veiled hat. She looked at us and smiled a queer smile. It was like she was expecting to find us in there. She disappeared for a moment and returned holding an empty candy box. I was about to pass dead away when a voice called out down the hall, 'Mildred, where are you, Mildred?'

"'I'm giving candies to the children,' the tiny lady replied.

"'It's time to go, Mildred. The flowers are all fresh now.'

"In a flash, I remembered the tiny lady. It was old Mrs. Lackland. She used to always give us candies when we were children.

"'Quick, hide!' I shouted under my breath.

"Kaye and Amy ducked behind two curtains. Scuff, Brian, and I dove behind the desk.

"'We have to go now, Mildred,' the voice said, approaching the door. 'See, Officer Schnepp is waiting to lock up the house.'

"I looked over and there was Officer Schnepp of the village police standing right outside the window. You could see his gun and holster and the stripe going down his pants. I closed my eyes and prayed he wouldn't look in.

"'Oh Tiffy, dear, the children are hiding,' Mrs. Lackland complained. 'Come see if you can find them.' And then she added in a whisper, 'I think they're behind the desk.'

"Brian, Scuff, and I stopped breathing. I think our hearts stopped too. We were like three frozen dinners.

"'Next week, Mildred, we'll find them next week. You'll miss afternoon tea if we stay any longer.'

"Up the hall the footsteps went. The front door opened for a few seconds and slammed shut. The lock bolt clicked in place. Just as soon as they were down the steps, we took off out of there like singed cats. Up the front stairs, down the back stairs, into the cellar, and out the window.

Did you ever go back in?" the new kid asked.

"Not on your life!" I shook my head, "the place gave me bad dreams for a month."

"I sure would like to explore that old place," he said, gazing through the trees toward the house. "You sure you wouldn't go back in?"

"Well...maybe. But I wouldn't go in there at night for a million bucks."

The Tree House

The two of us turned and continued along the path. "By the way," I said, "my name's John—John Hoffman. What's yours?"

"Buzzy Fancher."

"Buzzy! What kind of name is that?"

"My real name's Leslie but everyone calls me Buzzy—it's a nickname. Mom named me Leslie after my grandfather, but Dad said it's a girl's name so he started calling me Buzzy."

"Where do you come from?"

"Walton."

"Walton! No kidding! My dad was born and raised in Walton. He says it's a tough town. He used to deliver papers over on Stockton Avenue. He got beat up about once a week."

"It's not so tough anymore, just a railroad and a bunch of farmers."

"I used to visit my grandparents in Walton. They had a house on Townsand Street. Grandpa was a telegrapher for the railroad. Then he retired. He and Grandma came to live with us."

"You ever go to the skating rink?"

"Yeah, once a long time ago. It was a birthday party. Sheri Phillips invited our whole class. Her dad's rich. He owns the Buick garage. We went around and around in circles for about two hours listening to some fruity organ music. Every time you'd knock someone into the wall or break through the girls, this skinny four-eyed creep with a whistle would blast you. He made Scuff and me get off twice. Skating on the streets is better. There's no rules. Besides, Mom says I have to be in high school before I can go down at night."

"I used to go over every Friday and Saturday night and skate till midnight. The rink was only a block from my old house. Girls came there from all over. I had a girl-friend from Sidney."

"Your mom let you stay out till midnight?"

"Sure."

"And you had a girlfriend?"

"Well, sort of. Her name was Tish Lavern. We some-times skated together. One time she was even going to let me kiss her. We went out behind the rink but all her friends snuck around trying to spy on us. She got gig-gling so bad we had to go back in."

"Girls are like that, silly and always clinging to each other like a bunch of puppy dogs."

"Do you have a girlfriend?"

"Naw. I don't much care for girls. Too many other things to do—sports and stuff. I've got a big chemistry set too. I've been working on gunpowder so I can make my own fireworks."

"You're going to make your own fireworks? Wow, that's great! If you need any help testing them, let me know. I'm an expert at lighting fuses."

We emerged from the thick overgrowth of the Lackland estate into a wide grassy clearing along the river bank.

"This is my backyard, and there's the tree house," I said pointing to the limb of a giant willow hanging high over the water. Just beyond a crotch in the limb rested a large box-like structure with a smaller box on top of it. There were no windows but a trap door was visible in the floor.

"We didn't build it, the Honeywell boys did. They lived here before us. We only added the lookout on top. Come on, I'll show you."

Up the ladder boards nailed along the limb I climbed. In spite of the half dozen spikes in each, they were still wobbly. At the top, I pushed open the trap door.

"I've got to get another padlock on this door," I said, "Scuff dropped the old one in the river. Now anyone can get in."

I pulled myself up through the square opening into the tree house. Buzzy followed.

"Shut the door and latch it—just in case Scutter and his cronies are still wandering around. There's matches in the coffee can on the beam over your head. Light a candle. I'll open the lookout door."

Once a candle was lit and the lookout door open, it was light enough to see inside. Buzzy and I sat down on an old green rug and pulled up some cushions. It was real cozy. Comic books, candy wrappers, soda bottles, and candle stubs littered the floor. Baseball bats, hockey sticks, BB guns and fishing poles were stuffed in the corners. A collection of hubcaps hung from the rafters.

Magazine cutouts covered the walls. Most were of athletes and cars, but I'd put up a poster of a German V-2 rocket and Weed had put up a swimsuit calendar from Otto's Wrecker Service.

Buzzy checked it all out and relaxed against the cushions. He was pretty much as I'd remembered him the day the family moved in: short and sturdy, ruddy skin, blond hair that looked like it had been cut with a bowl, round friendly face and mischievous blue eyes. We were both dressed in blue jeans and plaid sport shirts, but his shirt was so dirty from the fight that I couldn't tell the colors. Then I noticed he was only wearing one sneaker.

"What happened to your sneaker?" I asked.

"It came off during the fight. The kid that was eating the candy bar stuck it on a stick and threw it into the river."

"Maybe it's still afloat," I said jumping up. "If it got caught in the current after the spillway, it'll be in Hamden by now, but if it stayed in the shallows, we should see it coming down."

I took an ancient pair of binoculars off the wall, climbed into the lookout, and scanned the river up toward the bridges. At first all I could see was a few branches and a bottle, but shortly a white sneaker appeared, bobbing up and down about twenty feet from the bank.

"There she blows," I shouted, "afloat and just beyond the Sloans. Grab two poles. We'll fish her out."

I climbed through the lookout door to the tree house roof, then lowered myself to a limb that extended far out over the water. Buzzy followed with two fishing poles. He handed one to me and together we started out over the river holding our arms up for balance. Below, the water was deep and muddy brown. It always got muddy after heavy rains."Careful," I said. "This old tree's mossy and slippery."

41

At first it was easy going, but toward the end the limb got skinnier and began to creak and bend. When we got to where we figured the sneaker would pass, we sat down and let our feet dangle over the water. I closed my eyes and took a deep breath. It was a wonderful feeling sitting out over the river—almost like drifting on a cloud. Warm sunlight played through the willow leaves. A gentle breeze rippled the water. Along the bank birds chattered in the brush, and grasshoppers hummed in the thick rye grass.

Buzzy and I sat in silence for a few minutes, taking in the sounds and smells of the river. I began to daydream and imagine myself flying low over the Amazon River in search of the lost city of the Incas. The beautiful daughter of missionaries has been kidnaped by the local natives and is being held in the city. I have volunteered for the dangerous mission of finding her. Suddenly a stone head as big as three barns rises out of the jungle carpet, its giant ruby eyes sparkling in the sun. I quickly bank my Curtiss seaplane and head for a crocodile-infested cove. But as the plane drops, it is met with a hail of poison arrows. Black smoke begins to pour from the exhaust. Frantically I pull back on the joy stick but it is too late. The motor has stalled. I slam into the murky water tearing off the right pontoon. Now my only escape is through seven thousand miles of hot, infested jungle. All I have for protection is my lever-action Winchester repeater. Then I see a clearing along the shore, and in the clearing, tied to a stone idol and surrounded by ferocious native warriors, is the girl. She is helpless and exhausted. My plane is drifting toward the clearing. I'll have to distract the natives. The flare gun! They've never seen a flare before. I pull the gun from my emergency kit and... "Say, John, who are those guys that keep starting fights with me?" Buzzy interrupted.

"Huh?" I sat up with such a start I almost slipped off the limb.

"Who are those guys that keep starting fights with me?"

"Oh yeah...those guys. They're a gang from up on Meredith Street and Cuddyback Avenue. They call themselves the Truckers. The four that waited for you after school are Turk McGraw, Roy Scutter, Jake Bonner, and Bertie Grimes. McGraw, Scutter, and Bonner are the big three in the gang. Bertie just tags along. When there's nobody better to pick on, they beat up Bertie. Roy is the leader. He's the tall, lanky one with freckles and sandy hair. Don't fool with him. He's tough—and smart too. Turk's the fat kid you poked in the nose on the playground. He's been in the ninth grade ever since I can remember and picks on everyone. Jake Bonner's the skinny one with the front tooth missing and a scar along his jaw. He's always smiling, but he's the meanest one in the gang. Last year a kid came to school whose family sharecropped on the flats. Jake slowly destroyed him. He pushed him into the lockers, knocked his books all over the halls, and tripped him up on the stairs. The kid didn't dare go to the bathroom. All of us felt real sorry for him, but we couldn't do anything. He'd be sitting in the cafeteria and as soon as the teachers weren't looking, Jake would throw a dish of jello or pudding at him. Nobody dared sit with the kid. He always smelled of food. I was glad when the family moved on."

"Don't you guys ever fight back?"

"Mostly we give them plenty of room and stay clear of Meredith Street."

"Hey!" Buzzy gave me a nudge. "Here comes my sneaker. Put your line down."

We lowered our hooks and sinkers to the surface of the water. Slowly the sneaker floated under the limb. I swung my line across it, but the hook slipped off. Buzzy swung his line and the hook caught a lace.

"Got her!" he exclaimed. He quickly reeled up the sneaker. After unhooking the lace and removing the stick, he wrung out the water and pulled it on his foot. I could tell he was real pleased to get it back.

The two of us rested the poles in our laps and sat watching the swirls of muddy water beneath the limb.

"Who are the other guys in the Trucker Gang?" Buzzy asked.

"Let's see," I said, scratching my head. "There's Luke Scutter, Roy's brother. He was with Roy on the playground. He's tall and got blond hair. They call him "Knuckles"—and for good reason. Billy "Bones" Lord is the black kid. Billy's got the tips of two fingers missing on his left hand. He blew them off with a cherry bomb. That's why they call him "Bones". He likes to come up behind you, twist your arm behind your back, and jam his finger stubs in your ribs. It practically knocks the wind out of you."

"Who's the short wiry kid with the shaved head and tattoo?"

"Gideon Spickey. Gideon's the fastest one in the gang and all muscle. We'd have been in real trouble if he'd been chasing us today. He hangs around with Frank Fano. Fano's a real animal. They call him "Bull.""

"I've seen Spickey and Fano together at the skating rink. They're always bumping into people and starting fights. Fano's dark with shaggy brown hair. He sort of looks like a tree stump with arms and legs."

"That's him, and he ain't much faster. But don't let him get hold of you!"

"That makes eight. Any others?"

"Some little kids but they don't count."

"Don't you guys have a gang?"

44

"Well, sort of. There's a bunch of us downtown guys that get together on weekends. We either meet here or in a shed behind O'Keefe's barn. We have a secret camp on an island behind the railroad yard too. Sometimes we raft down and spend the night there."

"Do you have a name?"

"You mean like the Truckers?"

"Yeah."

I shook my head.

"Great. Let's organize and call ourselves the River Rats!"

"The River Rats?"

"Yeah! The River Rats. My Uncle Mort told me about a gang called the Missouri River Rats. They built a raft and lived on the Missouri River. They were pirates. They had all sorts of adventures."

"Okay with me," I said, giving a shrug, "but we'd better discuss it later. Someone's coming on the path. Let's head for the tree house."

More Trouble

As we started back along the limb, the shouts and footsteps grew louder. By the time we reached the lookout, I could make out the voices of Turk McGraw and Bertie Grimes.

"It's the Truckers again. They're chasing someone," I said, feeling my heart begin to pound.

Buzzy and I dropped down through the lookout door and locked it behind us. Buzzy relit a candle while I opened the trap door in the floor. Then we stuck our heads out to see who was coming. After a few seconds, there was a sudden crashing of brush at the border of the Lackland estate, and two boys broke into the clearing. It was Weed Shaw and Scuff O'Keefe. They bolted across the clearing and jumped to the tree house ladder.

"Door's open!" I shouted.

There was more crashing of brush, and Scutter, Bonner, McGraw, and Bertie spilled into the clearing. They stopped and looked up at the tree house. Weed and Scuff were almost up the ladder. Buzzy and I still had our heads stuck through the trap door.

"Hey!" Jake yelled with a bigger-than-usual grin on his face, "it's Bozo Hoffman and his new girlfriend, Fuzzy-Wuzzy. Just who we've been looking for!"

Turk took an apple from his pocket and flung it at the tree house. It hit the wall and splattered.

"See that apple," he grunted, "that's what I'm going to do to the two of you. You two are dead meat."

"Better come down now and take your medicine," Roy said. "It's going to be a lot worse if we have to pull you out of that tree house."

Weed and Scuff scrambled through the trap door. I slammed it shut and set the latch. The boys collapsed on the floor.

"They chased us all the way from Bender's gas station," Scuff said gasping for breath. "Weed was helping me with deliveries. We came out of the station and they were waiting around the corner by the john door. They'd have jumped us if Mr. Bender hadn't seen them and warned us."

Weed cleared the hair from his face. His forehead was damp with sweat. "I didn't expect to see Truckers on Elm Street. Something must have stirred them up."

"They were after me and Buzzy," I said.

"You and who?"

"Me and Buzzy. This here's Buzzy," I motioned with my head. "They jumped him by Gundy's barn. I helped him get away."

The two boys sat up and looked at Buzzy. Weed's handsome face lit up with a big toothy grin. "You're the new kid across the street from John. You hit McGraw in the nose on the playground. Too bad you didn't do the same to Bonner. I'm Barney Shaw. Call me Weed."

Weed thrust his hand forward and Buzzy shook it.

"This ugly kid next to me is Dennis O'Keefe. He's your neighbor, if you didn't know. We call him Scuff."

Scuff smiled and shook Buzzy's hand.

"Been meaning to get over and meet you, but Dad's had me busy at ..."

Before Scuff could finish, there was a loud bang against the side of the tree house, then another and another.

"What's that?" Buzzy exclaimed sitting up.

We looked at each other in bewilderment. Suddenly a rock broke through the wall and rattled across the floor.

"Rocks! They're throwing rocks," Scuff howled. "Someone could get hurt. No telling what those idiots'll do."

A second rock broke through. It whizzed by Buzzy's ear. The four of us dropped to the floor and covered our heads. Outside I could hear the Truckers laughing and joking.

47

Rocks continued to bang against the walls for a long time. Then the rocks stopped and it was quiet.

"Think they left?" Weed whispered.

"Don't know," I said.

"Shhh," Buzzy held up his hand, "someone's coming up the ladder!"

I put my ear to the floor and listened. Buzzy was right. The ladder boards were creaking. Shortly the creaking stopped and it was quiet again.

Scuff gave me a worried look. "What do you think they're up to?"

"Don't know," I said. "It'll take a lot more than rocks to get into this old tree house."

"Maybe they're on the roof."

"Maybe."

"I'll see what's up from the lookout," Buzzy said, crawling over to the ladder.

"Don't get hit by a rock," I cautioned.

Buzzy climbed up into the lookout and slowly opened the trap door. After a brief pause, I heard him drop to the roof.

"Look!" Scuff pointed at the trap door. "They're trying to break through!"

I turned and saw the latch was bowed almost to the breaking point.

"Weed, quick, get on the door!" I yelled.

Weed was sitting next to the entrance. He jumped on the door and it bumped back in place.

"Bust it in, Turk!" a voice shouted outside.

Just then the lookout door banged shut and Buzzy dropped down.

"They're all on the ladder," he said. "They've got a log for a battering ram. Turk and Jake are up at the top."

Bam! Bam! Bam! came a series of blows to the door. They were so hard that Weed bounced off the door onto the floor. He sat up and rubbed his backside.

"Man, that hurts," he muttered.

Bam! Bam! Bam! came a second series of blows. The latch and hinges were almost torn out of the floor. Hubcaps in the ceiling began to clang together, and the candle on the floor fell over.

Scuff grabbed my arm. "We're trapped. We'll have to exit the lookout and swim for it," he cried.

"Not without first giving these guys some grief," I said. "Weed, grab a cushion and get back on that door. See if you can keep it shut for another minute. Buzzy, there's a gallon paint can on the shelf behind you. Bring it over to the trap door. Scuff, get your knife out and open up the screwdriver blade."

Buzzy grabbed the can and slid it over to the door. Weed was back on the door bouncing into the air with each blow. He looked slightly seasick. I took the can and held it while Buzzy pried at the cover with Scuff's knife. When the cover finally popped off, we beheld a thick enamel paint the color of chewed bubblegum.

"Yuck," Buzzy said, pursing his lips, "putrid pink. Where'd you get this stuff?"

"From Grandpa. Grandma bought it for the bathroom back when they were fixing the upstairs apartment. Grandpa couldn't stand it. Said it reminded him of a laxative his aunt used to give him as a kid. So he gave it to me."

"Quit the gab, you morons, and do something!" Weed hollered. "This door is killing me."

"Okay," I said, "listen up. When Weed gets off the door, you pull the latch, Scuff, then Buzzy and I'll dump the paint."

Scuff and Buzzy nodded. The three of us quickly surrounded the door.

"On three. Ready...one, two, three!"

Weed slid off the door as Scuff pulled the latch. We held our breath. The log struck the door hard, sending it flying open with a crash. Buzzy and I lifted the can and turned it upside down over the opening. Ga-gluck, gluck, gluck, went the paint. "Eeeeyaaaa!" screamed the surprised boys below.

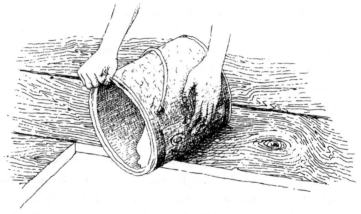

The four of us peered through the opening. Turk was directly under the door and had gotten the worst of it. He looked like a marshmallow sundae. The others were splattered but had managed to jump clear. As we watched, Turk started blindly down the ladder, slipped on a paint-covered board, and plunged into the river. He hit with a tremendous splash and disappeared under the surface in a pool of pink foam. Seconds later he rose from the bottom looking like a great bleached whale. His friends stared open-mouthed at him. Slowly Turk lumbered up out of the water wiping paint from his face. His eyes were tiny black slits and his jaw was set tight. He grabbed Bertie by the shirt and flung him headfirst into the river. Then he looked up at the tree house, shook his fist in the air, and yelled, "You guys are going to get it! I'm going to be waiting for you!"

"Come on up, you beedie-eyed blimp!" Buzzy taunted. "We got lots more paint!"

Buzzy was bluffing. We only had the one can.

"Let's get out of here," Roy said. "We'll deal with the dinks later."

The three of them started up the river path. Bertie scrambled out of the water and followed at a safe distance.

We watched until they had disappeared in the overgrowth of the Lackland estate, then closed the trap door and relaxed on the rug and cushions.

"Close call," Scuff sighed. He pulled a brush from his back pocket and began restoring his flattop.

Weed rattled around in a tin box until he found a cob pipe and lit up a wad of corn silk.

"Buzzy says we should start our own gang," I said. "We've got to stop letting the Truckers push us around."

"But they're a whole lot tougher than we are," Scuff shook his head. "Luke Scutter can handle any two of us."

"So we form a gang and let them know we stand together," Buzzy spoke up. "If they mess with one of us, they mess with all of us."

"Yeah," Weed sat up excitedly, "we'll get all our downtown friends to join. We'll sign our names in blood like Tom Sawyer and Huck Finn. We'll show the Truckers we mean business."

"First we'll make a list of members," I said, picking a pencil stub and paper off the floor. "Let's brainstorm. There's the four of us plus Amos, Fats, and Mickey Harrington."

"How about Okie, Tweets, and Hicks?" Scuff suggested. "They'll probably join."

"Who are Okie, Tweets, and Hicks?" Buzzy asked.

"Okie's the big kid that climbed in the window with me this morning," I said. "His Uncle Anton was driving the pickup. Okie's real name is Owen Blanchard. He lives up at the top of Franklin Street with his mom. His father ran off when he was a kid so he pumps gas at Ridley's garage to help support the family. Tweets is Ben Laney. He's the short, skinny kid with the big mop of hair. He always sits in the front row in class."

I stopped for a moment and gave a sigh. "Then there's Stanley Hicks."

"Yeah, poor old quaking Stanley," Weed chuckled, "scared of his own shadow."

"I know who he is," Buzzy said. "He's kind of tall and gawky, stutters when he talks. He sat in front of me today in class."

"That's Stanley," Weed nodded. "We can skip him and Tweets. They're a couple of flaming whiffs."

"Oh yeah?" I glared at him. "Stanley's okay. We used to play together when we were kids. And Tweets is real smart. He's got more brains in his little finger than you've got in your whole head. If it weren't for him helping you with math, you'd still be in the seventh grade."

"Yeah, Weed, if brains were gunpowder, you couldn't blow dust out of a teacup," Scuff laughed.

Weed dropped his pipe, pounced on Scuff, and began stuffing his head between two cushions. "You'd better take that back," he cried.

"Get off, Shaw, you overgrown ape!" Scuff howled.

"Let him go," I said grabbing Weed by the arm. "We have to finish this list."

The two boys settled back against the cushions. Scuff's face was bright red and his long nose slightly bent. Weed was grinning as usual.

"Tweets is in," I continued. "He and Okie are best friends. Okie'd never join without Tweets, and we need

Okie. He's the only downtown kid the Truckers are scared of. We'll have to take a vote on Stanley."

"What about Tony DeVito, Fritz Beamer and Joe Sweeney?" Buzzy asked. "I met them at DeVito's soda shop just before school started. They live around here—right?"

Weed, Scuff and I shook our heads.

"Yeah, they live around here but you can't trust them," I said. "The Truckers hang out at the soda shop Friday nights. Tony's friendly with some of them. He gives them free sodas when his dad's not around. Beamer and Sweeney are Tony's best friends. Beamer's okay but Sweeney'd sell out his own grandmother for a pack of gum."

I looked at the list and began adding up the names. "There's nine of us, not including Stanley," I announced. "We'll outnumber the Truckers."

"Hey, if we're going to form a gang, we have to have a name. What are we going to call ourselves?" Scuff asked.

"The River Rats," Buzzy quickly responded.

"Buzzy's uncle told him about a gang that lived on a raft on the Missouri River," I explained. "They called themselves the River Rats."

"Yeah, the River Rats, that's a great name," Weed said. Scuff nodded his approval.

"Let's get everyone together Saturday morning," I said. "We'll show Buzzy the camp on the island, then we'll raft down and explore the old woolen mill on the flats."

The three of them agreed.

"I've got to get going," Scuff said, starting for the door. "I've still got deliveries to make."

"Wipe off the ladder," I said, tossing him an old sweatshirt.

He dropped down through the trap door with the sweatshirt.

53

Buzzy stood up and knocked some of the dirt out of his trousers. "I'd better get going too," he said. "I've got to change these clothes and wash up or Mom'll know I been fighting. She said I'd have to stay in all weekend if I got into any trouble in school."

"I'd better get going too," Weed said. "It's almost supper time. Dad'll need help with the milking."

The three of us climbed through the trap door and started down the ladder. Scuff had already disappeared.

"I've got to remember to put a lock on this door," I said pulling it shut behind me, "especially now that the Truckers know about the tree house. Maybe Grandpa's got one in the barn."

Once on the ground, the three of us headed up through my backyard toward Elm Street. The sun was already low in the western mountains. Little did we suspect it was the last time we'd ever set foot in the old tree house built by the Honeywell boys.

Chapter 2. NIGHT RAFTING

A Note From Christina

AFTER MY EVENTFUL FIRST day in school, the rest of the week passed quickly. Buzzy and I spent most of our free time talking with friends and making plans for the River Rats. The Truckers pretty much ignored us. Whenever I met Jake Bonner in the halls, he would give me his usual strange smile, and Roy, Turk, and Bertie acted like nothing had happened—although I had an uneasy feeling they were up to something. On Friday the girls in our class announced a bake sale for recess the coming Monday to raise money for a dance and hayride. Christina invited everyone to her house on Sunday afternoon to help bake cookies and cakes. My friends and I groaned and made faces at the thought of baking cookies, but during history class Fay Bibbins passed me a note. It read: "Please come to my house Sunday. We can decorate cupcakes together. p.s. Bring your new friend, Buzzy. Bunny thinks he's very cute." It was initialed C.W. C.W.—Christina Wetzel? At first I figured it was one of Dennis O'Keefe's stupid jokes. Then I glanced across the room at Christina. She smiled and gave a little questioning nod. I almost fell into the aisle. It was for real. Christina Wetzel wanted me to decorate cupcakes with her. I was overwhelmed with a sudden blissful vision of Christina and me sitting next to each other at her kitchen table tracing little hearts in pink butter frosting.

"John Hoffman, stand up and list three products of the state of Connecticut," Miss Gromley snapped from the front of the classroom. I had the feeling someone was yelling at me from the far end of a tunnel.

"Huh?" I replied.

"Th-ree products of the state of Connecticut, John."

I slowly rose and cleared my throat. Teachers sure had a knack for ruining beautiful moments.

"Well," she demanded.

"Uh...oil...beans...cotton," I stammered.

"Oil, beans, and cotton," she repeated scornfully. "We are discussing the state of Connecticut, not Texas or Louisiana. Sit down and pay attention. I don't want to see you gaping about the room again."

There was a titter of laughter as I slumped back into my seat, but I didn't care. I was wondering how the minutes, hours, and days would ever pass until Sunday afternoon.

Ghost In The Storeroom

That night a terrific electrical storm drove through the valley. Enormous black clouds darkened the sky, great booms of thunder rumbled among the mountains, lightning flashed about the town, and rain fell in torrents. Shortly after the storm began, the village fire whistle sounded, and it sounded twice more before the storm ended. I knew the dangers of lightning especially to the local farmers. Sometimes it killed livestock, and sometimes it started fires. In fifth grade I was staying overnight with my friend, Nils Petersen, when his family's dairy barn was hit. We had just sat down to supper. Outside it was starting to rain. Suddenly there was an explosion like a hundred shotguns going off, and the side of the house lit up bright as day. Nils and I were knocked back from the table. Mr. Petersen and Nils' older brother Erik raced out the door for the barn. When they reached the yard gate, the front corner of the barn roof was already ablaze. There was nothing to do but try and save the livestock. By the time Nils and I pulled on our boots and ran out, the fire had swept through the hayloft and ignited the upper two floors. The air was filled with sparks and a strange electric smell. Mr. Petersen shouted at us to get the cows out of the barn. Burning shingles

57

and boards were falling everywhere. The cows panicked and refused to leave their stalls. We had to throw feed bags and a loop of rope over their heads and pull them out. The Delhi and Franklin fire departments arrived to find the whole barn ablaze. Flames rose a hundred feet into the air. The firemen hosed down the house, tool shed, and chicken coop but watched helplessly as the barn burned to the ground. Only the livestock and a tractor were saved. All the hay and machinery burned. Mr. Petersen quit farming after that and went to work for the county.

I lay in bed with my window open listening to the rain and thunder and watching the eerie flashes of lightning reflect off our neighbor's birch trees. For a long while I could hear the wail of sirens as the fire trucks raced out the Andes Road. I usually enjoyed the violent Catskill Mountain storms, but tonight I was concerned with the river and our plans to raft to the island and explore the deserted woolen mill below the railroad yard. The river was already swollen from last week's rains, and the added runoff might make it impossible to navigate the Steele Creek rapids. We'd have to give up our rafting plans.

As I lay pondering the Steele Creek rapids I thought I heard a noise in the upstairs hallway. Then came a faint tap! tap! tap! on my door.

"Who's there?" I called out.

The door opened and something shuffled in. At first I couldn't tell what it was, but then a flash of lightning revealed my little sister Karen in her long flowered nightshirt and furry slippers.

"What's the matter with you?" I asked.

"I'm scared of the storm."

"Oh gosh, Karen, go back to bed!"

"No! I'm staying with you."

"Go bother your big sister."

"She's asleep. Please get my sleeping bag. I'll sleep on the floor."

"I'm thinking about important things, Karen. I haven't got time for dumb little sisters who are scared of a little thunder and lightning."

Her face started to pout and I knew she was going to cry.

"Okay! Okay!" I grumbled, climbing out of bed, "I'll get the stupid sleeping bag and you can sleep on the stupid floor. Where is it?"

"In the storeroom."

Once out of bed I tried to turn on the light but it didn't work. I looked at my clock and it had stopped too. 'A tree must have fallen on the wires or maybe lightning hit a transformer,' I thought to myself as I stumbled across the room.

Karen was standing just inside the door with a somewhat impish look on her face. I gave her a gentle rap on the head and went into the hallway. The storeroom was only a few yards down the hall, but the hall was dark and cluttered with furniture. I slid my hand along the door frame and then reached down for the knob. I was surprised to find the door ajar. It was usually kept closed to keep the cat out. I pushed open the door and found it pitch black inside. Even the lightning couldn't penetrate the heavy shades over the windows. Raising my hands in front of my face I began to feel my way along the wall to where Mom stacked the sleeping bags. Suddenly there came a low moan from somewhere in the room. I stood motionless and listened. It stopped. Maybe it was Puffles our cat. I turned and searched the darkness. Goose bumps began to break out on my arms. I remembered old Andy Burr who fished the river at night telling me that ghosts sometimes get restless during thunderstorms and wander about. Slowly I backed toward the door. The moan started again and a light caught my eye. Then a shimmery green figure rose up from a pile of boxes. I stood frozen in terror. The figure rose higher and higher and the moaning got louder and louder. I knew I had to run but my legs just wouldn't move. Then my big sister Kaye's head popped over the top of an old silk sheet. She was standing on an old suitcase holding a flashlight under her chin.

"You look like you've seen a ghost, brother dear," she said, laughing and bugging her eyes at me.

Karen entered the storeroom. She was laughing too and clapping her hands.

I started to breathe again.

"I wasn't really scared," I said, trying to act calm, "just surprised. I figured it was one of those ball lightning things."

"You were too scared!" Karen howled and danced about.

"Shut up, you little fake," I yelled reaching out to grab her, but she disappeared in the dark and quickly reappeared clinging to her big sister.

"You kids quit banging around and get to sleep!" a loud voice called from down the hall. It was Grandpa.

"We'd better get to bed," Kaye whispered, "or Grandpa 'll wake the house."

I stomped out of the storeroom and returned to my bed. I couldn't believe my sisters had played such a stupid trick on me.

"I'll get even," I muttered under my breath. "Just wait till Kaye has one of her fancy high school parties and they turn down the lights and start smooching on the couch. I'll cook up a ghost they'll never forget!"

I lay down again and listened to the gentle tapping of rain on the roof. The thunder had quieted and before long I fell asleep.

The Missing Tree House

Saturday morning! Glorious Saturday! Two whole days free of books, blackboards, stuffy grammar, and dismal fractions. I was up before seven and even beat my father to the breakfast table. Buzzy gave a yell at the back door just as I was starting my second bowl of granola.

"Come on in!" I shouted.

Up the back stairs he ran and burst into the kitchen. His face was flushed with excitement. Blond hair flew in every direction.

"Let's get going," he panted. "The storm's passed through. It's beautiful outside."

"I have to finish my cereal first," I said.

"What kind of cereal is that?" he asked, dropping into a chair.

"Granola," I replied.

"Granola?"

61

"Yeah, Granola. Oats and nuts and dried fruit. Mom makes it. She says it's healthy, so I have to eat it."

"Don't you ever eat Sugar Pops or Frosted Flakes?"

"Only when I stay overnight at a friend's house."

"Let me try some."

I pushed the granola jar across the table. Buzzy took a handful, ate it, and dipped in for seconds. "Pretty good," he said munching loudly. "You got a glass?"

I pointed to the cupboard. He took down a large glass, filled it with orange juice, chugged the juice, poured a second glass, and took another fistful of granola.

"Gosh, don't they feed you at home?" I exclaimed.

"Just supper," he shrugged. "The rest of the time I'm on my own. Say, what are we doing this morning?"

"The whole gang should be here," I said. "Everyone on the list has agreed to join—even Owen Blanchard."

"You mean Okie the hillbilly?"

"Yeah, but don't call him hillbilly to his face if you know what's good for you. He can get plenty rough. One time Jake Bonner was teasing him on the playground— snapping his suspenders and calling him a clod and a hayseed. Okie finally got mad and gave Jake the worst licking in the history of the school. Bonner had a black eye for three weeks. But most of the time Okie's real friendly. He wouldn't hurt a flea."

"Great," Buzzy said, chugging the second glass of juice. "Let's get going."

We tossed our dishes in the sink, and the two of us exited down the hall stairs.

Outside the air felt warm and fresh in the morning sun. I could smell Grandma's lavender phlox clear across the yard. Puffy white clouds drifted overhead, remnants of the night's thunderstorm. Reilly, our back yard robin, was busy feasting on stranded worms. The grass was still wet, so Buzzy and I tossed our sneakers and socks onto the back porch and rolled up our pant legs.

"We'll have to check the river," I said as we started down the stone path along the barn. "It may be too dangerous to raft through the Steele Creek rapids. The island is just below the rapids. We can still get to it from the railroad yard, but we'll have to go around by the Walton Road. We've got a couple of rafts hidden behind the Co-op Creamery. The deserted woolen mill's about a quarter mile further down river on the flats."

"Why can't we get to the railroad yard by the river path?" Buzzy asked.

"We have to cross Steele Creek. Normally it's no problem, but after a storm it really whips up. Years ago some kids tried to wade across after a storm and one of them was washed out into the rapids and drowned. You have to cross at the Elm Street bridge."

"Let's build a rope bridge across the creek," Buzzy's face lit up, "or maybe string a single rope so we can cross hanging by our hands."

I liked the idea of a rope bridge and began thinking about all the rope Grandpa had stored up in the barn. We could make a terrific bridge with it—wooden slats and woven handrails just like in the Tarzan movies. But I wasn't sure Grandpa would be willing to donate his rope.

Behind the barn we stopped at Grandma's raspberry patch and picked a couple of handfuls of berries, then passed through a birch grove into the orchard. Old apple and pear trees were scattered across an expanse of green lawn. To the left of the orchard along the border of the Lackland estate lay Grandpa's vegetable garden of corn, sunflower, potato, and winter squash. To the right along the border of Thompson's field ran a tall wire fence thick with grape vines. The whole lower yard smelled of sweet ripe grapes. At the far end of the orchard, surrounded by tiger lilies and a stone patio, was the goldfish pond. Puffles sat at the edge watching the fish.

"Boy, this sure is some backyard," Buzzy exclaimed. "Back in Walton we had just enough grass for two lawn chairs and a pitcher of lemonade. You could put a whole circus out here."

I laughed at the thought of a circus in the backyard: elephants stomping around in Grandma's primrose and peonies. She'd have a fit. Probably chase them right into the river. Grandma wasn't afraid of anything.

We passed the fish pond and entered a scrubby field that ended at the river. We hadn't gotten far when Buzzy suddenly stopped and scanned the willows ahead.

"Something's wrong," he said. "The tree house is gone!"

"Aw, you're looking at the wrong tree," I scoffed.

"No, I ain't," he cried and took off running straight for the big willow overhanging the river. I ran after him. As we got closer, my heart began to pound faster and faster. The tree house wasn't at all visible—but maybe the storm had dropped a limb on it and covered it up. When we finally reached the foot of the tree and looked up, my heart felt like it was going to drop right into my feet.

Except for some floorboards and the trap door which hung open, the tree house was gone. I stared at the empty tree in disbelief.

"Come on," Buzzy said grabbing me by the arm. "Let's go up and take a look."

We climbed the ladder and pulled ourselves up through the trap door onto the remaining floorboards. Scrawled on the boards in red paint was the message:

Underneath it was drawn a skull with an axle through it and truck tires on either end of the axle.

Buzzy and I sat in silence. I drew up my legs and dropped my head into my folded arms. I felt sick all over. The tree house had been my second home. I'd slept nights in it since I was a little kid, spent whole weekends in it with my friends playing games and reading comic books, fished from the roof, spied from the lookout, and kept my most prized possessions scattered about the walls. Now everything was gone. For the first time I knew how Mr. Petersen felt when he stood watching his barn burn to the ground.

The River Rats

"Buzzy! John! What happened? Where's the tree house?" voices called from below. It was Weed and Amos.

Buzzy leaned over the side. "The Truckers wrecked it. They threw everything into the river."

Amos' mouth fell open. "Even the baseball bats and gloves and hockey sticks?"

"Naw, they probably took all that stuff home with them."

A high-pitched call rose and fell, and Mickey and Fats appeared from the orchard. The two boys ran up to the willow tree and stared in amazement at the remains of the tree house.

"Where'd it go?" Mickey asked.

"The Truckers wrecked it," Weed replied. "They threw most of it into the river."

"They threw the tree house into the river?" Mickey repeated as if in a daze.

"It must have been just before the storm hit last night," I called down. "Scuff, Fats, and I were playing cards on the roof right up till it started to cloud over. They could never have torn it apart in the dark. They must have been hiding on the Lackland estate watching us. Lucky they didn't throw us in with it."

Fats cast a weary glance into the dense overgrowth of the Lackland estate. "It's kind of scary having the Truckers stalking around Elm Street. They used to stick pretty much to Meredith and upper Main. They could be watching us right now."

As Fats finished speaking there was a sudden rustle of brush and two figures emerged near the river path. Fats didn't wait to see who they were. He turned and ran full speed for the orchard.

"It's just Tweets and Okie," Mickey called after him.

Fats stopped and slowly trudged back.

"Fats you're the biggest scaredy-cat in the whole county," Weed scoffed. "I'll bet you even check under the bed at night to make sure Jake Bonner isn't hiding there."

"Yeah, Weed, and you're the biggest meatball this side of canned spaghetti," Fats grumbled back.

Tweets and Okie hurried over to the willow tree. Okie was dressed in his usual bibbed overalls, tee shirt and work boots. His hair was uncombed and his thick glasses streaked with dirt. Tweets was about half Okie's size and looked like he'd just been scrubbed and put out on the front steps to dry. His white shirt and brown chino pants were starched and spotless. His mop of blond hair was neatly parted in the middle.

"Did it get hit by lightning?" Tweets asked.

"It got hit by the Truckers," Mickey replied.

"The Truckers wrecked it?" Okie scratched his head. "How come?"

"Because John and Buzzy poured a can of paint over Turk McGraw's head," Weed spoke up.

"They did what?" Tweets gasped.

"Roy, Jake and Turk trapped us in the tree house yesterday. Turk tried to bash in the trap door so Buzzy and John poured a can of paint on him. He fell into the river."

"Jeez," Tweets shook his head, "that's practically a declaration of war!"

"They were asking for it," Weed shrugged.

Buzzy and I were still sitting up on the floorboards. "Come on," Buzzy said giving me a nudge, "no use moping around. We've still got the shed behind O'Keefe's, and the camp on the island."

We got up, climbed down the tree, and joined the others.

"Are you sure it was the Truckers?" Okie asked.

"Yeah, they left a message on the floorboards," I replied. "Go up and see for yourself."

One by one the boys went up to look at the message scrawled on the floorboards. Then we all sat down on the river bank and waited for Scuff. He arrived shortly and, after being informed of the destruction of the tree house, sat down with us. Scuff was as upset as I. We'd played together in the tree house since we were little kids. He hung his head and cursed the Truckers under his breath.

Mickey finally stood up and faced the rest of us. His tee shirt sleeves were rolled up to show off his muscles. Affecting an air of importance he said, "Now that we're all here, let's get down to business. The Truckers have been causing us grief for years. Now they've even invaded Elm Street where they're perpetrating all sorts of atrocities!"

A big groan went up from the group. Mickey read a lot and liked to show off big words.

"What's a 'perpetrating'?" Okie asked.

"What's an 'atrocity'?" Weed added.

68

"Skip the five dollar words," Fats grumbled. "We came here to form a gang, not listen to some dumb speech."

Amos stood up and faced Mickey. "Who made you leader of this gang anyway, Mick? It was John and Buzzy who had the idea."

"Yeah, Mick, you're always trying to run things," Scuff joined in.

"Okay, okay," Mickey said holding up his hands, "I'll make it short. The Truckers are bigger and tougher than we are—except maybe for me and Okie; but if we band together and let them know we're going to fight back, they'll leave us alone. We've all pledged to join the River Rats. That means we'll stick together no matter what against the Truckers. Agreed?"

Everyone nodded or said yes.

"To make it official, John and Buzzy have drawn up a charter."

I stood up, pulled a crumpled paper from my rear pocket and opened it up.

"It says that if a River Rat is in any sort of trouble or gets captured or attacked by the Truckers, the rest of us will come to his rescue. It says that our secret sign is a circle with the initials RR in it. It says that our secret handshake is to press twice with your thumb, and the other guy answers with three presses of his thumb."

"What do we need a secret handshake for?" Amos interrupted. "It isn't like I'm going to forget who Tweets or Scuff is."

"Yeah, but what if it's in the dark?" Scuff suggested.

"I sure as heck ain't going to go creeping around in the dark shaking hands," Amos laughed.

"Gangs always have secret handshakes," I said.

"I've got it! I've got it!" Weed exclaimed with a big grin. "You're all alone in the boy's john at school—except that someone's in one of the stalls. So you sneak up, stick your arm over the door and say, 'give me the secret handshake.' If he busts your arm you'll know it's a Trucker. Haw! Haw! Haw!"

The others laughed too.

"Okay, okay, we'll skip the handshake," I said turning the paper over. "On the back is a list of our names. We each have to write our initials in blood."

Another groan went up.

"Let's just use red ink," Scuff said.

"Or maybe we could blot our thumb print in ketchup," Fats recommended.

"Get serious, you guys," Buzzy said. "It's got to be blood, or we won't be a real gang!"

"How are we going to get blood?" Scuff began to look uneasy.

"Simple, Scufferoo," Weed chuckled, "stick your skinny nose over here and I'll put a fist in it."

"Maybe I'll put a fist in your nose," Scuff glared back at him.

Buzzy reached into his pocket and pulled out a pin. "Look," he said, "just prick your finger."

He stuck the pin into the end of his finger. A tiny bead of red blood appeared.

"Yaaaa! I can't look," Amos cried in mock horror and covered his face.

70

"Grab Tweets," Weed shouted, "he's going to faint."

"You're funny, Weed, real funny," Tweets scowled.

Buzzy put the piece of paper on the ground and made his initials in blood.

"Okay, who's next?" he said.

Mickey took the pin, pricked his finger and initialed next to his name. The others followed. When everyone had signed, I took the charter, folded it back up and put it in my pocket.

"We planned to raft to the island today," I said, "and show Buzzy the secret camp and maybe explore the old woolen mill below Sherwoods. But with last night's rain it's too dangerous to raft through the Steele Creek rapids. Even if we got through, we'd never get back up."

"We'd better forget about rafting and figure what we're going to do for a clubhouse," Amos spoke up.

"Yeah, what's a gang without a clubhouse," Tweets joined in. "Bertie Grimes has been bragging that the Truckers have three clubhouses."

"We've still got the shed behind Scuff's," Mickey said.

Scuff shook his head. "Dad's filled it up with boxes from the drug store. Besides, the place smells of chickens."

"I've got a better idea," I said, "let's rebuild the tree house—and this time put a lock on the door."

"Yeah! Great! Let's do it!" everyone exclaimed.

"Where are we going to get the materials?" Mickey asked.

"Grandpa's got a pile of old lumber behind the barn and tons of nails and tools upstairs. Weed and Scuff can take the rafts from behind the town yard and pick up any boards that washed into the cove. Fats, your uncle's in the roofing business. Can you can get him to donate a roll of tar paper?"

Fats moaned and lay flat on his back on the bank.

"What do you say, Fats, can you get the tar paper?" Mickey asked.

Fats didn't move. Mickey signaled to Weed. He and Weed each took one of Fats' feet and shoved him head-first over the bank into the river.

"You idiot jerks," Fats yelled splashing and spitting out water, "you got my shirt all wet."

"If you don't get that tar paper, you'll get more than a wet shirt," Mickey threatened.

"Get stuffed, Harrington," Fats grumbled, "I'll get the tar paper if I feel like it."

He climbed up the bank and stomped up the river path toward Kingston Street.

"I'm going with Fats," Amos said and ran after him.

We watched the two of them until they disappeared into the overgrowth.

"Take it easy on Fats," I said, "especially you, Weed. Sometimes you aren't so funny."

There was a long silence. Then Mickey jumped up and shouted, "What are we waiting for? Let's get moving!"

Weed and Scuff got up and started for Thompson's field. The rest of us headed up through the garden for the barn. I was feeling in good spirits again. This time we'd build a tree house the Truckers would never get into.

Rebuilding The Tree House

The whole day was spent working on the tree house. First the frame was rebuilt and carefully bolted to the limbs. Then a new lookout was constructed even higher than the old one. Once the lookout was finished, we started nailing down roof and floor boards. Little kids, dogs, and curious neighbors gathered to watch. Even Grandpa showed up. He sat on his old wooden wheelbarrow smoking a pipe and occasionally grumbling that a lot of good lumber was going up into that tree. About noon Mom brought a tray of peanut butter and jelly sandwiches down for us. Then Christina Wetzel, Fay Bibbins, Becky Chambers, and Bunny Reimes arrived with a basket of cookies and fresh lemonade. They'd been practicing for Sunday. Some of the cookies took considerable jaw work but the lemonade was great. They offered to help if we'd let them use the tree house. We said they could take one look inside when it was finished, but then it was off-limits to girls. With that they picked up their basket, turned up their noses, and strutted off up the river path.

By late afternoon the roof and floor boards were nailed down and the siding going up. Buzzy and I were nailing down tar paper on the roof when I heard Amos shouting below.

"What's the matter?" I yelled.

"We're out of wood. Okie's cutting the last piece."

I leaned over the roof. The pile of boards from the back of the barn and cove was gone.

"Any more in the cove?" I asked.

Weed and Scuff shook their heads.

I dropped my hammer and climbed down into the tree house. Only one wall had siding on it. Tweets pulled up the last board on a platform we'd rigged with a rope and pulley. Fats took the board and held it in place while Mickey nailed it to the frame. When he'd finished nailing,

Mickey stepped back and looked at the open walls. "We'll need a lot of lumber to cover these walls," he said.

"Yeah," I agreed, "we'd better have a meeting."

Buzzy, Mickey, Fats and I climbed down out of the tree and gathered with the others on the bank. We all stood for a moment admiring the half-finished tree house.

"It's a great job," Okie said thrusting his hands into his overalls.

"Yep," Buzzy nodded, "the Truckers'll have to dynamite this one apart."

"They won't have to dynamite anything," Mickey scoffed. "If we don't finish the siding, they'll just unscrew the lag bolts and drop the whole thing into the river."

"They aren't smart enough to do that," Scuff said.

"Oh yeah?" Tweets turned to Scuff. "Roy Scutter's plenty smart."

"It doesn't matter," I interrupted. "We have to finish the siding. Anyone got any ideas where we can get more lumber?"

"What about Salter's lumber mill," Amos suggested, "it's closed down and there's piles of lumber lying around."

"How will we pay for it?" I asked. "It'll cost at least thirty bucks."

"Offer Mr. Salter a trade. We'll clean the place up —stack wood, whatever he wants—in exchange for enough siding to finish the tree house."

Fats shook his head. "Old Mr. Salter's gotten a little crazy. Dad won't get near the place anymore. Salter rides around the deserted yard all day in his pickup. Keeps a double-barreled shotgun in his lap and two big dogs in the front seat with him. He wouldn't sell the lumber even if you had the money. You go asking him about trading and he'll blow your head off. He says there's Communists all around the town trying to steal his lumber. He told

Dad they were stealing it to build a secret airport up Elk Creek."

"An airport up Elk Creek," Okie laughed, "there ain't enough flat land up there to land a box kite."

We stood quietly for a while.

"Any other ideas?" I finally asked.

My friends shook their heads.

"Too bad Salter is crazy," Mickey said. "We could have floated the lumber right down the river."

Buzzy's face lit up. "Where's the mill?" he asked.

"About a quarter mile above the bridges," Mickey replied. "The yard runs from the river to a three-story building on Main Street. It's right across from the Delaware National Bank."

"We've got rafts, right? Let's raft up the river tonight and take what we need. No sense letting good lumber go to waste."

"Yeah!" Weed exclaimed. "Salter won't be around the yard at night. He'll never know the difference."

Amos looked concerned. "It's stealing. We could get in a lot of trouble."

"Yeah, it's stealing," I said, "but what else are we going to do? Like Weed says, Salter'll never know the difference."

"I'm with Weed, Buzzy, and John," Scuff spoke up. "Who else is going to raft up tonight? What about you, Mick?"

"I don't like stealing, but I guess it isn't really so bad if the wood's going to rot anyway. I'll go."

Okie shook his head. "I have to work at the bowling alley tonight. I'm setting a double league for couples."

"Count me out," Tweets frowned. "It's stealing and stealing is against the Bible."

"Oh holy, quaking Moses," Weed groaned and rolled his eyes, "are you some kind of religious freak, Tweets?"

Tweets ignored him.

"What about you, Fats?" I said.

Fats gazed out across the muddy, swollen river. "It looks dangerous," he said. "How'll we ever to get up the rapids under the bridge?"

"We'll stay in the shallows close to shore and walk the rafts if we have to. Better we have too much water than too little. We won't have to worry about grounding."

"Okay, count me in," he sighed.

"That leaves you, Muss," Mickey said. "Are you with us?"

Amos shrugged. "I wouldn't miss rafting up river at night for anything, but I won't set one foot on Salter's property. Like Tweets says, it's stealing."

"That makes seven of us," I said. "We'll take four rafts. Tell your parents we're sleeping out in my backyard. Meet here at dark."

Everyone agreed and pitched in to help carry the nails and tools to the barn. Then we disbanded for supper.

Rafting Up River

Buzzy and I arrived early to bring up the five rafts. It was a cool misty night along the river. Frogs croaked among the reeds, and katydids droned in the trees. Overhead a broken covering of low gray clouds moved slowly up the valley. Beyond the clouds the sky glowed bright with stars.

First we laid out our sleeping bags and then walked in silence down the river path, listening to the sounds of the night. Behind the town storage yard we pushed through a narrow thicket, slid down the bank and waded into the reeds. Ahead in the starlight we could see a circle of rafts tied to the corner of a protruding bridge span. The span had washed down in a flood and lay buried in the mud. It was a great place to hide the rafts except for the eels that hunted the murky shallows. They sometimes slithered by my legs, sending shivers up my spine.

The two of us climbed up on the span, untied the rafts and retied them into a train. We then jumped aboard the lead raft. Long saplings were stored under the deck for poling. We each took a pole and pushed hard into the muddy river bottom. The rafts rocked gently as they began gliding through the reeds. Ahead in the dark, bats swooped and flitted over the water. A curious water snake lifted its glistening head from the water and quickly disappeared.

"We'll stay close to shore," I whispered. "Keep an eye out for snags."

It was difficult staying close to shore, especially at night. Each raft had two inflated inner tubes tied underneath to keep the deck above water. Sometimes the tubes got hung up on sunken limbs or trash. Sharp metal or wood could cause a blowout. The worst was fence posts with pieces of barbed wire. If we lost a raft we'd have to put three on one raft and that would make it just about useless for carrying lumber. But in the deep water beyond the reeds the current was dangerous. We couldn't chance moving further out and getting swept into the river.

Gradually Buzzy and I made our way through the reeds and entered the quiet shallows along the shore. Enough light shone through the clouds to navigate the snags. We soon reached my backyard. The others had arrived and started a small fire on the bank.

"Hello!" Buzzy called out.

"Hello!" they called back.

We broke into the light of the fire and poled toward shore.

"Everyone here?" I asked.

"Yeah," Amos answered, "plus we've got Tob."

"Tobin Harrington?"

"Yeah, I brought my kid brother along," Mickey called out. "We'll make him an honorary River Rat for tonight. He can help with my raft."

Tobin was two years younger than Mickey. The brothers could almost be taken for twins except that Tobin was shorter and not as rugged.

"Okay with me," I nodded. "Let's get going. It feels like rain."

Buzzy and I grounded the lead raft on the bank. Weed and Amos got on the one behind us and began untying the lines. Fats and Scuff took the third raft, and the Harringtons the fourth.

"Where's the extra rope?" Amos asked.

"Here," Weed said and tossed a coil to him.

"What about flashlights?" Buzzy said.

"We've only got one. Amos has it," Scuff replied.

Amos pulled a long metal flashlight from inside his jacket. He turned it on and flashed it out across the river. We watched in silence as the light fell across the black, churning water. The river was running deep and swift. We'd be at its mercy if we got beyond poling depth.

"I don't like it," Scuff said, shaking his head. "It looks a lot worse at night. Maybe we should wait a few days."

"I'm with Scuff," Fats spoke up. "It's looks dangerous out there."

"And let the Truckers tear down what we've built?" Weed cried. "Everyone in town knows we're rebuilding the tree house."

"We didn't have any trouble bringing up the rafts," I said. "Just stay close to shore. Amos, only use the flashlight in an emergency. We don't want people getting suspicious."

"And no yelling or loud talking," Mickey added.

We lifted our poles, pushed off from the bank and headed single file upstream toward the Kingston Street bridges. The clouds overhead were closing and threatening rain. The only light came from two streetlights at either end of the bridges. I was beginning to feel uneasy about getting up river in the dark. We had to navigate three dangerous areas before the mill: the left fork spillway, the bridge rapids, and the stone channel overflow. Maybe Fats and Scuff were right. Maybe we should wait a few days. I glanced over at Buzzy. He was whistling quietly to himself as he poled and didn't seem the least concerned. Behind us the other rafts were coming out of a light mist. Amos, Weed, and Mickey were pretty fearless; they'd want to go on even if it stormed. I wouldn't say anything unless we got in trouble at the rapids.

In spite of the strong current working into the shallows, it didn't take us long to reach the spillway of the left fork below the twin bridges. The river split above the bridges and joined again below. In the middle lay an island half covered by an old wooden factory building. The left fork was wide and shallow and useless for rafts or boats. Most of the water came down the right fork through the rapids. But with the river running high there was plenty of water coming through the spillway. We'd have to be careful not to get swept out into the river.

Buzzy and I dropped off the raft as we started across. The water was over my knees and moving with tremendous force. One slip on the rocky bottom and we wouldn't have a chance.

"Wait up!" Amos called from behind.

He threw us the end of a rope. The others were tying the rope to their rafts to form a chain. Once the rafts were secured, we slowly guided them across the spillway. I had to force my pole into the river bottom with each step to keep from being pushed over. I wondered how we'd ever get rafts loaded with lumber back across the spillway. Maybe we'd have to pull them across one at a time using the rope.

As we approached the island, the current slackened and the rocks gave way to sand. Ahead I could hear the rush of water as it churned and drove through the rapids. It was a terrifying sound in the night. Buzzy was listening too. I wondered if he was half as scared as I was.

We rounded the island and entered the foamy water along the flooded banks. "Untie the rafts," I said, "and stay close in as possible."

Cautiously Buzzy and I led the way up toward the bridges. Sometimes I'd feel solid bottom, and sometimes I'd drop into a hole or sink into the mud. A few yards to our right huge swells rose from the river sending clouds of spray into the dim street light overhead. Toward the far shore a tree swept down by the storm lay wedged in the rocks. Around it the water swirled and splashed furiously as if trying to strip away the limbs. The sight of the battered tree made me shudder. The river wouldn't treat us any better if we strayed into the current.

"Pull to the right!" Buzzy yelled as we came under the bridge.

We had worked our raft up to the head of the rapids. I braced my feet and pulled hard on the deck line as Buzzy pushed. The raft slid over a ledge of submerged rocks and dropped into a backwater pool dammed in by the concrete bridge support. There was still a current but the bottom felt solid. I held the raft against the support while Buzzy helped pull the other rafts over the rocks. Fats and Scuff came up last. They were both pretty exhausted, so we rested for a few minutes. Once they felt better, we passed under the bridge and entered the stone channel. The stone channel was so named because of the high stone walls that contained it. The walls had been hand laid of flat field stone in the late eighteen hundreds to protect the village from flooding. In some places the walls rose twelve feet above the water. The only break was at the overflow where the left fork branched off. There a rock and gravel overflow dam had been built to control the water and prevent boats from being drawn in and grounded in the shallows. Crossing the dam might prove the most dangerous part of our upstream journey. Normally one could walk across but during storms the water sometimes rose to a height of several feet. If the water was as high as at the spillway, we'd have to turn back.

"Keep to the wall," I called to the others as we started up the channel. The channel was at its narrowest and deepest just above the bridges. Here the current was swift and unpredictable. Toward the middle, swells rose up from the river bottom in what looked like great rolling snakes. Such a snake could easily flip a raft and drag us under.

Buzzy pushed the raft against the wall with his pole while I pulled on rocks to ease it upstream against the current. As we crept along the wall in the dark listening to the churning of the water, I felt as if I were in a strange dream and maybe I'd wake up and find myself at home in bed.

"Help! Help! We're getting swept out!" Fats and Scuff suddenly cried.

Amos snapped on the flashlight and swung the beam onto their raft. They were already a good pole length into the river.

"Push into the wall! We'll throw you a line!" Mickey yelled.

Fats and Scuff tried to pole but lost bottom. The raft began to spin in the current. Mickey grabbed a coil of rope. Holding one end, he hurled the coil as hard as he could. The coil unraveled and dropped across the raft. The two boys fell on it and Tobin and Mickey pulled them back to the wall.

"We'll tie your raft between Amos' and ours," Mickey said.

Fats and Scuff looked pale and frightened. We were all pretty shaken. If Mickey's throw had been off, they would have been lost to the river.

"Do you guys want to turn back?" I said.

They shook their heads.

After securing the raft to Mickey's and Amos', we continued up the channel. The river gradually widened and the current slackened enough that we were able to pole the rafts. Along the approach to the overflow the river was running almost a foot below the high water mark on the wall. It was a good sign. The overflow should be passable. I was beginning to feel we were actually going to make it up river to the mill.

Buzzy and I arrived at the overflow ahead of the others. We drove our poles deep into the mud to hold the raft against the wall and waded out onto the narrow dam.

The water was below our knees but swift and the rocks covered with slime. We'd only gotten a few feet when I motioned to go back.

"It's too slippery," I said shaking my head. "If we lose our footing, we'll wash into the left fork."

"Let's try on our hands and knees," Buzzy suggested.

"Okay," I said, "but we're going to get soaked."

As Buzzy tied one of the raft lines around his waist, I pulled the poles out of the mud and secured them to the deck. He then dropped to his hands and knees and started across. I did the same and followed behind the raft. The raft pulled hard in the current, but we were able to hold it back. The worst of it was getting our knees torn up and an occasional mouthful of dirty river water.

The other three rafts waited at the approach. Once we were across, they followed one at a time. Amos and Weed came last.

"That's the worst of it," Mickey said holding Amos' and Weed's raft against the wall while they climbed on. "From here on it's duck soup."

"Duck soup or pneumonia," Fats muttered, wringing out his shirt.

"What about getting back down, Mick?" Scuff asked. "It's going to be ten times as hard handling loaded rafts—unless you've got a helicopter hidden around here."

I could tell Scuff's Irish was up.

"Easy," Mickey shrugged, "we'll be moving with the current. Just stay close to shore."

"Yeah, and what about the rapids?"

"Relax, Scuff. We'll deal with the rapids when we get there—all right?"

"We'll deal with the rapids when we get there," Scuff mocked. "Wish I was a jerk-head genius like Mick and knew everything."

Once again we formed the rafts into a line and moved

up river. Along the far shore a cluster of weathered houses came into view, their foundations built close to the channel wall. The few that showed lights had shades drawn over the windows. Low voices drifted across the water from the porch of a one-story shack. We poled close to the wall and crouched as low as possible, but someone must have seen us because I heard one man say, "There's some damn fools out fishing the river. Must be looking to drown."

After the houses we came to a bend in the river. The trees and brush along the wall gave way to a large clearing. Overhead the last patch of starlit sky closed, and drops of rain began to fall.

Salter's Lumber Mill

"Mill's dead ahead," Mickey called as he brought his raft into the lead. "Listen up, everyone! John, Buzzy, Weed, and I will climb the wall and look for lumber. The rest of you stay with the rafts. Watch out the current doesn't take you out. We'll send the lumber down."

"We're going to sit in this stinking river in the rain while you guys—the heroes of the River Rats—do all the exploring!" Scuff shouted.

"Hold it down, Scuff," Amos said. "We didn't come this far to have you wake the town."

"Look!" Scuff waved his hand in front of his face. "I can hardly see my hand. How're we going to see lumber dropping off the wall?"

"I've got a flashlight, remember?"

"If we use the flashlight, someone will see us for sure."

As he spoke a pickup truck rumbled up Delaware Avenue toward Bridge Street, its headlights lighting the trees on the far bank. We all didn't move until it was out of sight.

"See what I mean?" Scuff muttered.

"What else are we going to do?" I said. "We'll have to chance it. Use signals. Three owl hoots when the coast is clear and two for trouble. You can come up the wall with us if you want, Scuff."

"Forget it," Scuff shook his head. "The place is probably crawling with ghosts."

"There's the sluice," Amos said pointing to a wooden structure that hung out over the water. "We're at the mill."

We poled the rafts into a line, passed under the sluice, and pushed into the wall. Fats jumped to our raft and drove a pole into the river bottom to hold it in place. Buzzy and I felt along the wall until we got a good foothold and began climbing. Mickey and Weed started up from the other rafts. The rocks were damp but sharp and easy to climb. I was more worried about getting bit by a startled rat or snake than slipping off.

The climb went quickly. Once on top we gathered behind a pile of rusted and overgrown machinery to look over the back of the yard. I knew the yard well. When I was a little kid my parents rented a house on upper Main Street near the county buildings. I used to bring my wagon down to the mill, and the workmen would load it with scrap wood. Even then the place was pretty run down. I remember one of the workmen showing me a deserted apartment where the floors were warped like wrinkles in a blanket. Grandpa told me the mill had been active right into the 1930's. Trees were lumbered off the mountains as far up as Stamford and floated down river to be cut into lumber. At that time Salter's Mill employed and housed over a dozen families. A rail link with the railroad yard was even planned. But then in 1936 a hundred-year flood hit the valley. The West Branch rose two feet over the walls and swamped the mill. The buildings and machinery were badly damaged and two big steam engines destroyed. Mr. Salter never recovered from the loss. The mill reopened but only to gradually sell off the lumber. The logging works was abandoned.

"See anything?" Mickey whispered.

"Only bats," Buzzy replied.

Weed gave me a nudge. "You know the place, John. Where do we go?"

I pointed to a long, two-story building leaning ominously on its sunken foundation. The roof line rose and fell like the back of some strange beast. The walls were buckled and bent.

"See that building," I said. "It's the main shed. That's where logs were pulled in from the river. There's a saw blade in there as big as Buzzy, and a steam engine as big as a garage. There's all sorts of tracks and cables and gears—like a giant erector set."

"Skip the tour," Mickey grumbled. "Where's the lumber?"

"Hey! We should come here some night—maybe Halloween —and crank up that steam engine," Weed said, ignoring Mickey. "Throw a few logs in the boiler. Bet old crazy Salter would really think the Commies had landed."

Mickey grabbed Weed by the shirt. "We're wondering when you're going to land, Weed. Now cut the babble and get serious."

"There's a road that runs the length of the main shed," I continued. "Then it cuts between two barns connected by an overhead loft. After that it turns into the upper yard. That's where the lumber's stacked. We could go through the buildings, but the floors are all rotten—lots of fallen beams and broken glass. It's better to stay with the road."

"Let's go," Buzzy said.

We circled from behind the pile of machinery and headed into the yard. I led the way through the brush and rubbish to an overgrown gravel road. We followed the road up to the barns with the overhead loft. It looked like a huge tunnel between the barns and was pitch black. Weed stopped and held up his hands.

"I hear something," he muttered.

The rest of us stopped and listened.

"Just the rain," Buzzy said.

Mickey gave Weed a push to go ahead.

"Cut it out," Weed said pushing him back. "If Salter's waiting for us in there, we're all dead."

We stood quietly studying the dark passageway ahead. The more I stared, the more I was certain I could see forms moving in the dark.

"I'll go first," Buzzy said. "I'll give a low whistle if it's okay."

He walked up the middle of the road and disappeared in the dark. Shortly a faint low whistle came from the other end.

"Let's go," Mickey said, and the three of us followed at a run.

Past the end of the barns the road made a sharp turn and we entered the upper yard. It was bordered on the right by a row of ancient crumbling apartments and on the left by lumber sheds. Walls in the apartments had collapsed, exposing empty rooms and severed floors. At one wall a bathtub hung in space supported only by pipes. At another a closet door opened to a two-story drop. Mattresses and broken furniture lay scattered about the foundations. The sheds were worse. Most of the roofs had fallen in, pushing out the walls. The racks of lumber lay warped and broken. Everything smelled of damp and decay.

Above the yard on a steep hill rose the offices and stores that fronted upper Main Street. The buildings were outlined against the night by the town streetlights. The tallest building was the three-story Salter Building. It stood dark and foreboding except for a single dim light in a back room on the third floor. The light gave me an uneasy feeling. I could imagine old crazy Salter sitting up there with a spyglass, watching his mill.

"Help yourself!" Buzzy met us with boards tucked under both arms. "Great stack back there," he motioned with his head, "tongue and groove siding."

We hurried to the pile, tossed off a few weathered scraps, and began tucking the ten foot boards under our arms. But we soon found the boards were awkward and hard to balance.

"It'll take us all night to carry boards like this," Mickey said. "Let's stack them up and two of us'll carry the stacks together."

It was a great idea. For the next half hour we stacked and carried lumber to the wall. Buzzy and I worked as a team, and Mick and Weed worked together. Getting boards down the wall proved slow and difficult. Without the flashlight it would have been impossible. But the light was a hazard. Sooner or later someone would see it and wonder what was going on. If the police saw us from Delaware Avenue, there'd really be trouble. We had to work fast so we split up: Buzzy and I made trips into the yard while Weed and Mickey handed boards down the wall to the rafts.

"A couple of more trips and we're loaded," I said to Buzzy as we entered the upper yard. It was our sixth trip in. We stopped at the pile of siding and began stacking up boards. The stack was almost ready when Buzzy unexpectedly dropped the end of the board we were lifting. He stood upright and cocked his ear toward the street.

'What's the matter?" I said, feeling goose bumps breaking out on my arms.

"I heard a motor start up," he whispered.

I listened and heard it too. "Sounds up...," I started to say, but before I could finish, a pickup truck roared from behind the apartments at the upper end of the yard. It traveled about thirty feet in the dark, skidded to a stop, and the headlights went on. I stood paralyzed in the sudden light. It was like staring into a flashbulb.

"Run!" Buzzy yelled and he pushed me so hard he almost knocked me over. I spun around and took off. We both headed down the road for the river. The truck engine screamed and the wheels tore into the dirt. Between the barns we raced, through the pitch black tunnel and out the other side. The truck was gaining fast, its headlights throwing eerie shadows across the buildings and trees. Buzzy was normally faster than I, but as we approached the main shed we were running neck and neck.

"Push off! Push off! Salter's coming!" we yelled at the top of our lungs.

Two splashes came from the river. Mickey and Weed had jumped off the wall. The truck rammed through a pile of lumber sending boards flying about the yard, then screeched to a halt, steam hissing from the radiator. The doors banged open and loud barking burst from the cab. I tried to run faster, but everything felt in slow motion. The river seemed miles away. "Stop, you Commie thieves!" a high-pitched voice yelled.

Two blasts like large firecrackers went off and pellets whizzed through the air all around us. I felt sharp stings in my back and legs but kept going. The dogs crashed through the brush and grass. They were almost on us. I expected sharp teeth to sink into my leg any moment, but suddenly the earth was no longer under my feet although my legs were still moving. I felt myself falling into the darkness. There was a loud splash, and cold, swirling water enveloped me. When I came up I heard Buzzy calling. He was clinging to a raft a few yards away.

I swam to the raft and together we pushed it out into the current.

Two big dogs ran along the wall barking and leaping about. Shortly the outline of a small skinny man appeared. More shots went off, but the pellets splashed harmlessly in the water. We'd been caught in the swift current and swept out of range.

The Rapids

"Did you get hit?" Buzzy asked, his head bobbing in the water.

"Yeah," I nodded, "it really stings. Feels like I've got a pellet in my leg."

As I spoke the raft dipped into a small whirlpool and began spinning about. Waves of water rushed over us. We clung desperately to the platform until it had passed through.

"We've got to get out of this river," Buzzy said spitting out a mouthful of water. He gripped the deck and tried to pull himself up. The raft was loaded with lumber and began to tilt dangerously.

"Let go!" I cried. "You'll flip it!"

Buzzy dropped back into the water. "We couldn't control it even if we got on," he said. "We'd better swim with it."

"Let's try pushing it out of the current—toward the overflow," I said.

We worked our way around the raft and began kicking as hard as we could. It was a useless effort. Ten of us couldn't have kicked the raft out of the current. It was like a leaf in a storm drain.

"Better save our strength for the rapids," Buzzy said, gasping for breath. "We just passed the overflow."

As the channel narrowed, the current drove harder, and the top-heavy raft began to rock violently. We moved to opposite sides and hung on the lashings to try and stabilize the load. Up ahead I could hear shouts. The other rafts were trapped in the current too. Amos was yelling to stay with the rafts or they'd drown for sure. Scuff called to Tobin to cut loose the lumber or he'd capsize.

I pulled myself enough out of the water to see down river. The bridges loomed only a few hundred feet ahead. In the glow of the streetlights I saw the three rafts approaching the rapids. Amos and Scuff had almost managed to pole their raft to the pool beneath the concrete support, but the other two were in trouble. Weed and Mickey were clinging to the inner tubes of Fats' raft. Fats was straddling a stack of lumber holding a pole across his lap. The raft suddenly shot between two enormous swells, rose high on a third, pitched violently and flipped. The three boys and the raft disappeared in a cloud of foam and spray.

Tobin was alone on the third raft. The raft entered the rapids near the left bridge support. Tobin struggled to ground the raft in the shallows, but he fell among the loose boards on the deck and lost his pole. The raft spun into the current, accelerated through a swirling channel under the bridge and crashed into the tree at the foot of the rapids. Both inner tubes tore loose and the deck sank beneath the water. Tobin was thrown into the branches and pinned by the water.

I was filled with such fear that I almost panicked and let go. 'I can make it to the wall,' I thought to myself, but the wall stood thirty feet away and the water was black and seething. It was impossible. The only hope was to stay with the raft.

"See anything?" Buzzy said.

I hung my head. "Tob's trapped in the rapids," I muttered. "Mick, Weed and Fats are gone—flipped over. We should never have gone on the river tonight. We should never have gone."

"What about Amos and Scuff?"

"They're okay. They made it to the wall."

"Trouble ahead!" Buzzy yelled.

We were still in the channel. Suddenly the water began churning like a giant turbine. I felt a tremendous pull on my legs. The raft rose up on one edge, taking Buzzy with it, and cut into the water, falling on top of me. The lumber and deck pushed me under but I held onto the lashings. If I hadn't, the undertow would have quickly dragged me to the bottom of the river. The raft dove deeper and deeper. My eardrums ached and my lungs felt like they would burst. Water rushed into my nose making my head throb. It seemed like the raft would stay down forever, but it gradually rolled, and my head broke the water. I gasped for air. The raft rolled again and took me under. It came up at the head of the rapids, slammed into a rock, and began coming apart. I flailed blindly in the water and caught an inner tube. A foot kicked me in the stomach. My God! my leg is broken and bent double I thought, then I saw Buzzy's head and arms pop up on the other side. It was his foot. He looked half drowned but managed a faint smile as we dropped into the rapids.

We were swept with such force that I had to grip my wrists around the inner tube to hang on. Water poured over our heads; swells lifted and tossed us; the driving water pounded our limbs against rocks and dragged us along the stony bottom. I was sure we would die. Everything would soon get light and peaceful. The newspapers would tell about six boys drowned in the west branch of the Delaware River while attempting to steal lumber. What a terrible thing for my parents and grandparents, their only male heir dying a common thief. At least Amos and Scuff made it. They'd tell how we wanted to work for the lumber but were afraid of old crazy Salter. There'd be a big funeral. Christina would come and put flowers on the coffin. Maybe she'd be sad. Maybe she'd realize she liked me a whole lot more than she ever let on. Maybe she'd ...

Mr. Daniels

"John! You okay? John, wake up!"

It was Buzzy shouting. I looked about. We were through the rapids. I couldn't believe it. We really made it through hanging onto an inner tube. It was a miracle. I'd go to Sunday school every Sunday for the rest of my life.

"John, we've got to get out of this river. We'll never survive the Steele Creek rapids."

Everything slowly came back to me. We were still in the middle of river being swept down stream toward the Steele Creek rapids. The Steele Creek rapids were worse than the Kingston Street rapids. There Steele Creek drove into the river forcing the water through a rocky channel along the left bank.

"Get on my side," Buzzy called. "We'll push her to shore."

I swung around the inner tube next to Buzzy. Together

95

we began kicking as hard as we could and paddling with our free arms. But I was soon so exhausted I almost slipped off. Pulling myself back up, I looked over at Buzzy. He had stopped swimming too and was resting his head.

"We're finished," he sighed. "We'll never get out of this river."

The light from the bridges was receding in the distance. We were rapidly drifting into the dark, stormy night. I began to feel terribly cold and tired. Even my bones felt cold. I wanted to close my eyes and go to sleep, but knew I'd never wake up.

"Listen," Buzzy said, "it's the rapids."

Downstream I began to hear the low rumble of the Steele Creek rapids. It sounded like a gently purring motor. The motor suddenly got louder and louder—but we were still far from the rapids. A bright light flashed across the water and lit the inner tube. I gazed into the light as it crept closer and wondered what was happening. I'd remembered reading that when people die they sometimes see a bright light. Then I recognized the familiar chug! chug! chug! of the motor.

"It's Mr. Daniels!" I shouted. "He's coming to get us in his boat!"

An ancient wooden craft cut across the current following the beam of light. I'd seen it on the river dozens of times. It was a homemade boat powered by an old John Deere tractor motor. Mr. Daniels' father had built it and built it well. Once in a spring flood the boat had broken from its mooring, drifted into the Steele Creek rapids and lodged in the rocks. I remember Grandpa pointing to it and telling me it was Noah's ark. Only the rudder was damaged.

"Coming about," Mr. Daniels called as he swung the bow directly into the current, then pulled alongside us. Buzzy and I looked up in amazement as Weed, Mickey, and Fats leaned over the side to haul us in.

"You guys made it!" I cried.

Weed and Mickey pulled me in, and I collapsed into a heap on the floor. Fats and Mr. Daniels pulled in Buzzy.

"Who else is missing?" Mr. Daniels asked.

"Amos, Scuff, and Tobin," Fats replied.

"Amos and Scuff poled to shore above the rapids," I said. "They're okay. Tobin's caught in a tree at the foot of the rapids."

"Is he alive?" Mr. Daniels asked.

"I don't know," I said.

Mr. Daniels opened the throttle and headed up toward the rapids. He held a long flashlight in one hand which he shone back and forth across the water. The rest of us sat quietly in the boat. We were all praying Tobin was alive.

"This is as far as I can go," Mr. Daniels finally announced. We were about a hundred feet from the bridge. The motor was laboring hard, and Mr. Daniels was fighting to keep the bow pointed into the current.

"Come here, John," he motioned to me. "Take the flashlight up to the bow and shine it on the tree. Keep low and move slow through the boat."

I took the flashlight, carefully made my way to the bow,

and shone the light on the tree. Tobin was still pinned against the branches. His head and shoulders were out of the water, but he looked limp.

"Tobin! Are you okay?" I yelled.

He didn't move.

"Tobin! Do something! Show us you're alive!"

His left arm slowly lifted out of the water and dropped down again.

"He's alive!" Scuff screamed. "He's alive!"

Mickey covered his face and burst into tears.

"Looks like he's swallowed a lot of water," Mr. Daniels noted, "bit of shock too. We got to get him out of there quick."

"Get me to shore. I'll run to my house and call the fire department," I said.

Mr. Daniels shook his head. "We got to get him out of there right now."

Up on the bridge we heard shouting. It was Amos and Scuff. They were pointing at the tree. Mr. Daniels rubbed his chin for a few moments and then began backing the boat away from the rapids.

"Yell to those boys and tell them to meet us at the end of the island—by the spillway," he said.

I called out the message, and Amos and Scuff immediately headed for the island path. Once in deep water Mr. Daniels steered the boat toward the spillway.

"Which one of you is a good climber?" he asked.

"I am," Buzzy said.

"You pretty brave too?"

"Yeah, I guess so."

"Good. I'm going to give those two boys a coil of rope to carry up on the bridge. You go up with them. Tie one end around the bridge rail toward the middle. Tie it good and tight. Drop the other end into the water and let all the rope out. When it comes through the rapids, we'll take it into the boat. Then I'm going to steer the boat to line the rope up over that Tobin fellow in the tree. When I give a wave of my hand, you shimmy down and try and get him out. Understand?"

Buzzy nodded.

"Have a cup of hot cocoa first, you'll need all your strength."He handed Buzzy a small silver thermos.

Amos and Scuff were in the shallows when we arrived at the island. Mr. Daniels tossed over a large coil of three-quarter inch rope and told them to take it up on the bridge. Buzzy dropped into the water and followed. Once on shore, the three of them hurried up a narrow path along one of the concrete supports, climbed over the guard rails at the top, and ran out onto the bridge. Buzzy took one end of the rope and carefully tied it to the handrail. Scuff undid the coil while Amos lowered the loose end into the water. Quickly the rope washed through the rapids to our waiting boat.

"Tie it around your waist, John," Mr. Daniels said after I'd fished it from the river. "Then you other boys hold on so he doesn't pop out of the boat."

I tied the rope around my waist. Mickey and Weed gripped it in the bow with me. Fats held me around the chest and waist.

"Ready?" Mr. Daniels shouted.

"Ready," we answered.

He revved the engine and cautiously maneuvered the boat out into the river, letting it drift just enough to keep the rope taut. Once the boat was in line with the tree, he waved to Buzzy to start down. Buzzy climbed over the rail. He gripped the rope with both hands, lifted his legs and wrapped them around it, then slowly lowered himself out over the rapids. We watched in awe. It was a good twenty foot drop to the river. Down the rope he came until he almost touched the water. Mr. Daniels let the boat drift again and the rope tightened. Buzzy released his legs and hung by his hands. After a short rest he moved hand over hand along the rope until he was over Tobin. We could hear him yelling and see Tobin trying to grab his feet but the rope was too high. Mr. Daniels revved the engine. Buzzy dropped into the water to his knees. Tobin caught him around the waist, and Mr. Daniels slowed the engine. I felt a tremendous pull on the rope as the boat moved back with the current. Tobin and Buzzy rose almost a foot out of the water.

"Hold on, you guys!" I shouted, feeling myself lifted off the bow seat.

"We got you," Fats said.

Once more Mr. Daniels slowed the engine. The rope tightened, and suddenly Tobin and Buzzy popped out of the water like a cork from a bottle. They dangled in the air a few inches over the tree.

"Buzzy's shaking his head," Mickey called to Mr. Daniels. "He can't hold on. He's going to drop."

Mr. Daniels angled the bow toward the island and opened the throttle. The boat swiftly moved toward mid-channel. When the rope was over a deep chute he shouted, "Tell them to let go. We'll pick them up."

Before any of us could relay the command, Buzzy's hands slipped from the rope, and he and Tobin splashed into the current. As they swept by the boat, Weed, Mickey, Fats, and I leaned over the side and grabbed them. They were both so exhausted they could hardly swim.

"Throw off the rope," Mr. Daniels said once they were safely in the boat. "We're going to shore."

I untied the rope from my waist and threw it into the water. Amos and Scuff began pulling it back up on the bridge. The boat headed down river.

Sitting on the floor, I looked up and felt rain splashing

in my face. It had been raining since we arrived at the mill, but I hadn't even noticed. Then my legs began to shake, and I felt cold all over. My left shoulder ached terribly. Buzzy was sitting across from me, his head on his knees. He was shaking too. The skin on both his feet was raw and bleeding. Mickey had collapsed in the bow. One of his knees was so bruised and swollen he could hardly stand. Weed sat propped up against Fats. He had a wide gash along the side of his head and felt sick and dizzy. Tobin lay on the floor. Mr. Daniels had covered him with burlap bags to keep him warm.

The boat turned into a misty cove flanked by two giant willows. Mr. Daniels cut the engine and eased it up to a low dock. Amos and Scuff were standing on the dock with the coil of rope.

"You boys got here quick," Mr. Daniels said with a chuckle. "Good thing. Let's give a couple of these pirates a hand. Better start with this Tobin fellow. Get him home and in a warm bath."

Amos and Scuff climbed into the boat and helped Tobin to his feet.

"Can you walk?" Amos asked.

Tobin nodded.

They lifted him up on the dock. Then each one got under an arm, and the three of them headed for the street.

Fats helped Weed up on the dock. Weed was having a hard time keeping his balance.

"I'll walk him home," Fats said. "See you tomorrow."

Buzzy and I started into the bow to help Mickey, but he motioned us back. "I'll be okay," he said. He stood and swung himself onto the dock using his arms. Then he got up and limped out across the yard after Amos, Scuff and his brother. After bailing a couple of inches of water out of the boat and thanking Mr. Daniels, Buzzy and I trudged down the river path toward my backyard.

"Stop by and thank Miss Panky," Mr. Daniels called after us. "If it weren't for her hearing your shouts and giving me a phone call, you'd all been drowned."

A Talk With My Parents

When I got home, Mom and Dad were sitting at the kitchen table waiting. They looked at me anxiously as I came through the back hall doorway. I must have been some sight all soaked and shaking and reeking of fish from the burlap bags.

"We just got a call from Mr. Daniels," Dad said as I closed the door. "He told us you and your friends almost drowned in the river tonight. Whatever were you doing rafting on the river on a night like this?"

I gazed at the red and green flower patterns of the plastic tablecloth. Each flower petal was a thick, sloppy brush stroke.

"Well?"

"Getting lumber for the tree house," I muttered.

"Lumber for the tree house?"

"Yes, siding. We ran out of siding."

"Siding? From the Salter yard? You were stealing siding from the Salter yard?"

My eyes followed a cluster of stems and leaves until they disappeared under the sugar bowl.

"Well?"

"Yes. We were stealing it."

There was a long terrible silence. Dad stared at me, slowly shaking his head. I wished I could crawl into the tablecloth and disappear among the flowers.

"Go up and take a hot bath," Mom finally said. "Leave your clothes in the hallway."

By the time I got undressed and up to the bathroom, Mom had already drawn a full tub of hot water. After the bath she brought a mug of hot cocoa to my room.

"You and your friends were very lucky," she said after I'd finished the cocoa. "You'd better sleep late tomorrow. We won't call you."

As she turned off the light she reminded me to say my prayers.

Sunday Afternoon

When I woke the next day and looked at my clock it was almost four in the afternoon. The shade was drawn and what sounded like hail clattered against the window. I lifted the shade and was surprised to find the sun shining and Buzzy, Amos, Tweets, Fats, and Scuff standing in the side yard. They'd been throwing pebbles at my window.

"Come on down!" Buzzy yelled. "You've slept through the whole day.

"Yeah, Hoffman, you're getting lazier than a pet raccoon," Scuff grinned.

"Be down in a minute," I said. "Meet me out front."

In spite of a sore back and shoulder, I quickly dressed, raced down the stairs, and burst out the front door.

"Where's Weed, Tob, and Mickey?" I asked as I joined my friends. "Are they okay?"

"Mick has to stay off his leg until the swelling goes down," Scuff said. "Dr. Turner x-rayed his knee this morning. It wasn't broken but some stuff inside was torn up. He may have to be on crutches for a while. Tob's okay but he has to lay low for a few days to make sure he doesn't get pneumonia."

"What about Weed?"

"Concussion," Amos announced solemnly. "He'll be out of school for a week. His old man's plenty mad at us. He wouldn't even let me see him this morning. But his Mom told us we can visit when his Dad's not around."

"We can go up tonight around six," I said, "Mr. Shaw'll be doing chores in the barn. Then we'll stop and see Mick and Tob."

The others agreed.

Tweets stepped forward, reached into his pocket and pulled out a slightly squashed cupcake with pink frosting. "We just finished baking and decorating at the Wetzels," he said, handing it to me. "We had a great time. I must have eaten fifty cookies. Christina asked about you. I told her you camped out last night and probably forgot about the party. She spent the afternoon with Tony. Tony sent the cupcake."

My heart just about dropped into my sneakers. I'd slept right through the decorating party. I'd blown my big chance; and now Tony had moved in on Christina. Tony DeVito, the one kid in my class I'd never gotten along with. He was cocky and tough, and his father owned the only soda shop in the town. I looked down at the cupcake. Stuck in the frosting were tiny red candies that spelled out: 'MISSED YOU CREEP'.

I turned and chucked the cupcake as hard as I could into the thick brush along the Lackland estate.

"What'd you do that for?" Fats gasped.

I just shook my head and stared at the grass.

"Don't take it so bad, old buddy," Scuff said hanging his arm over my shoulders. "The way you act around Christina, you'd probably ended up with both feet in the frosting."

"Amos, tell John about the raft and old crazy Salter," Buzzy spoke up.

Amos laughed. "I went down to Wrenwick's Drug Store early this morning to get the Sunday paper. Mr. Salter was standing in the middle of a group of men telling how he and his two dogs fought off a Commie frogman attack last night. He claims there's a submarine hidden in the channel."

We all laughed.

"Then Fats, Scuff and I got together after Sunday school. We went back to the pool under the bridge. Scuff's and my raft was still there. We tied ropes to it, eased it down the rapids and poled it to your backyard. While we were unloading the lumber, Buzzy showed up. He went down to the cove to look for stray boards. He didn't find any boards but he found something better."

"I found another one of the rafts grounded in the Steele Creek rapids," Buzzy broke in. "It still has all the lumber lashed to it—enough to finish the tree house. If we can get rope from your barn, we can pull her to shore."

"Great!" I said, "but we can only get the rope if Grandpa's not around. He doesn't like me doing things on Sundays."

The six of us took off around the back of the house into the barn. Grandpa was nowhere to be seen. I unhooked two coils of rope from the wall and we exited the rear door for the river. Once there we split up. Buzzy and I climbed aboard the raft and poled it along the shallows while the others took the river path. I'd pretty much had my fill of the river, but I sure didn't want to lose the lumber. We met on the sand bar that formed the cove above Steele Creek. Buzzy and I tied one coil of rope to both inner tubes of the raft. Then Amos, Fats, Scuff, and Tweets eased us out into the river and down the rapids. The current swept us close enough to the grounded raft that we were able to pole up behind it. I was afraid we would jar it loose, but the raft held, and we were able to lash it to our raft with the second coil of rope. Our friends pulled from the shore, and we pushed hard on our poles. Slowly the two rafts rose up out of the rapids. Once in deep water they drifted across the river and grounded on the sand bar in the cove. Buzzy and I jumped ashore with the others and we all whooped and danced like Indians. We could now finish the tree house. I couldn't wait to tell Weed and the Harringtons.

Chapter 3. THE RAILROAD YARD

A Talk With Christina

THREE WEEKS HAD PASSED since the night rafting adventure. The tree house was finished with siding to spare and was even better than the tree house the Honeywell boys had built. Before, we'd had to open the trap door or climb up the lookout to see who was outside. Now we had portholes all around like a ship, and each porthole could be opened or closed by sliding a board. The trap door was solid oak and held shut by an enormous bolt lock Grandpa gave us. The lock didn't really work because the keys had been lost, but it sure looked impossible to break open. To get in all you had to do was move one of the floorboards a couple of inches. That was top secret of course. Above the tree house in the highest limbs of the old willow tree, Amos and Buzzy had nailed up a new lookout platform. It was pretty scary getting up to it, but we now had a clear view of the river path almost to the bridges. Mickey and I built a crude telegraph set out of nails, strips of galvanized steel flashing, bell wire, and dry cells, then strung wire up through the backyard to my room and across the street to Buzzy's house. Grandpa taught us enough Morse code to tap out simple messages. He'd once been a telegrapher for the railroad in Walton. If the Truckers were on Elm Street, we could quickly signal the tree house.

The inside was still sparse but we'd managed to pick two sofa cushions and a mangy bear rug off Ben Crow's garbage truck. The bear rug came complete with head, a mouth full of sharp white teeth, one glass eye, and fleas. Fats was searching for valuables in the mouth one afternoon and got his hand stuck in the teeth. We had to grease it with lard on a paint brush to get it out. All he found was a dead mouse and some acorns. Other than the rug and cushions, there was a new swim suit calendar from Otto's Wrecker Service on the wall, and a lone picture of Duke Snider ready to swing at home plate. We'd soon get more pictures, but the loss of the B.B. guns, fishing gear, baseball gloves, bats, and hockey sticks was pretty bad. It'd take most of my autumn leaf raking money to buy a new glove and hockey stick. I figured the Truckers had all the stuff stored at one of their hideouts on Meredith Street or Cuddyback Avenue. I even asked some of the little kids from that neighborhood about the Trucker hideouts, but they didn't know, or they weren't saying. Even if they had told me there wasn't anything I could do—unless maybe some of us snuck up there one night. I suggested it to the others, but only Buzzy was interested.

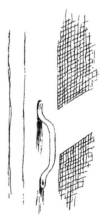

Christina Wetzel had pretty much ignored me since I missed the Sunday decorating party. I was hoping to get a chance to apologize, but every time I saw her, Tony DeVito was right there getting in the way. She was all smiles with Tony, and Tony was lapping it up like a puppy with its first saucer of milk. Whenever I got too close he'd cock his head and give me one of his "get lost" looks. It was all I could do to keep from pasting him in the nose. Bad feelings between Tony and me went way back. When I was about eight I started going to the back lot to play baseball. Tony was there too. I didn't know many of the older boys, but Tony did because they all hung out at his father's soda shop. I was a new kid so they'd gang up on me—push me around and call me carrot top or rooster because of my reddish-brown hair. Then they'd get Tony to start a fight with me. I could handle Tony, but the older boys made sure I always got the worst of it. If we were rolling in the dirt and I came up on top and pinned Tony, they'd kick me off or pull my hair and say I wasn't fighting fair. More than once I went home in tears—but I always came back. After a while I got to be one of the regular players and the fights stopped, but I never got over my dislike for Tony.

"You're wimping out," Scuff enjoyed reminding me at least once a day. "You're letting DeVito walk all over you."

"Oh yeah!" I'd reply angrily, "what am I supposed to do? I can't get near Christina. Tony's always with her. He even walks her home from school."

"You're just making excuses," he'd say shaking his head, "you don't have a chance. You're the class doof when it comes to girls. You've got to be cool like me and Weed."

Being cool like Weed and him meant hanging out in the doorway at nickel dances watching everyone else dance. I didn't usually listen to Scuff, but he did get me thinking. One night after supper I decided to go over and see Christina and explain about missing the party. I felt pretty confident going down Elm Street, but by the time I'd crossed the Kingston Street bridges I was as nervous as a treed cat. I must have walked by Christina's house a dozen times before I got up the courage to climb the stone steps to the porch and push the doorbell. Christina answered the door. She was wearing a white blouse, blue jeans, and brown sandals. Her dark red hair was pulled up in back. She seemed surprised and somewhat curious to see me. I stood there with my hands stuffed in my pockets, head bent, half looking at her and half looking at the screen door.

"I-I was just walking down Delaware Avenue," I stammered, "and thought I'd stop by and say I was sorry I missed the decorating party."

She smiled, then came out on the porch and took a seat on the steps. I sat down next to her. For a few moments we gazed out across the green lawn and graveled street toward the river. Trees and brush along the bank showed flecks of orange and gold. A silent evening breeze fluttered the leaves. The first stirrings of autumn were in the air.

"I was really looking forward to decorating cookies with you," I said. "We got into some trouble the night before. I was pretty wrecked Sunday—slept most of the afternoon."

"I know," she said. "You, Mickey, Weed, and some of the other boys were rafting. I heard you tipped over."

"Yeah, it was pretty dumb. The river was dangerous. We got caught in the current above the rapids. If it weren't for old Mr. Daniels and his boat, we'd have all drowned." I figured it was best not to mention we were stealing lumber.

Christina turned and looked at me. Her face seemed a shade pale. "That would have been awful, just awful," she said, touching my arm and giving a deep sigh.

Christina's touch was so unexpected I almost slid off the step. My arm was tingling all over. I figured I'd better play it for all it was worth. I'd show Scuff.

"Yeah, we'd probably never been seen again," I muttered. Buzzy told me that's what happened to a kid down in Walton. He was fishing off the Apex railroad bridge and fell in. The river was running high. It swept him clean away—down to Brooklyn and out to sea."

"Brooklyn? You mean Philadelphia."

"Yeah, wherever. They never found a trace of him."

"Please, let's not talk about the river anymore," Christina said. "It's making me shiver all over."

We sat quietly for a few seconds. To our left the sun was dropping among the western mountains leaving the sky a soft purple streaked with orange. Dots of crows drifted along the high ridges. The pastures and forests glowed a dusty blue.

"Does Buzzy like living here?" Christina asked.

111

"I guess so," I replied. "He sure has made lots of friends."

"Are you his best friend?"

"Yeah, I expect so. We spend all our free time together."

"Where did he get the name Buzzy?"

"He told me but it's kind of secret."

"I won't tell. I promise."

"Well, his real name is Leslie. He prefers Buzzy—says Leslie is a girls' name."

"Does he like the girls in our class?"

"Yeah, I suppose he does. He doesn't say much."

"Does he like Bunny? Bunny thinks he's very nice."

"I guess so."

"Does he like anyone special?"

"Maybe Melinda Johnson."

"Melinda Johnson in the ninth grade? How does he know her? She lives in Hamden."

"He sees her in the halls and at lunch. She even let him carry her books out to the buses last week."

"Ohh," Christina sighed with obvious disappointment. Bunny was one of her best friends.

There was a long pause. Christina rested her face on her hands. Her brown eyes gazed up into the evening sky from under their long, dark lashes. Then she turned to me and smiled.

"Do you ever feel you've lived before in other times and other places?" she asked.

"I spent the first three years of my life in Laurens just outside of Oneonta," I replied, "but the only thing I remember was sitting in a big flower patch and getting stung by a bee. Other than that, I've never been much beyond Delaware County."

"I don't mean here, in Delhi, and now. I mean ages ago. Do you ever feel like you've known people before you met them—maybe like Buzzy?"

I thought again. I'd taken an immediate liking to Buzzy, and I'd always disliked Tony. But what I remembered most was the first time I met Christina in the church meeting room. I could still see her standing there in her white satin dress and black polished shoes.

"Yeah, I guess I see what you mean," I said.

Christina looked up into the sky again. "I feel like we've known each other for such a long time."

"Yeah, since third grade."

"No, not since third grade... since Rome or Greece or maybe ancient India."

"India?" I blinked.

"Sometimes on nights like this when the stars are coming out, I can almost remember ages ago. I want so much to remember."

With her head still lifted to the heavens she took a deep breath and closed her eyes. I'd never seen her so mysterious. I sat watching as if in a dream. I was almost afraid I might remember too.

"Hello, John," Doctor Wetzel broke in with his thick Czechoslovakian accent. He was standing at the screen door. "Christina, telephone for you."

Christina turned and looked at her father. For an instant she seemed hesitant. Then she laughed and jumped up."It must be Tony," she said. "He usually calls about this time."

My heart sank. She and Tony were even talking to each other on the phone. Scuff was right. I didn't have a chance. I could never talk to a girl on the telephone. I wouldn't know what to say.

Just before disappearing inside Christina called, "Thanks for stopping by. See you in school tomorrow."

I shuffled down the steps and across the lawn. Inside I felt as empty as a stave barrel.

Saturday Morning Football

Tobin Harrington was still restricted after school and on weekends. It turned out he'd broken a couple of ribs when he got thrown into the tree in the rapids. Mickey and Weed were fully recovered, but Weed's father was still plenty sore at us. The World Series ended in late September with the New York Giants defeating the Cleveland Indians in a four game series. Most of us were Brooklyn Dodger or Yankee fans but we were still excited that a New York team won. With baseball over, the River Rats and other downtown boys began their Saturday morning football games. We played at MacKenzie's corner lot next to the First Presbyterian Church. The lot was the best football field in town. One end zone was a thick row of long needle scotch pine, and the other the main street of the town. Good running teams liked to strip off tacklers in the trees, whereas good passing teams used cars for interference. A goal line stand could tie up traffic for two blocks. After each touchdown we'd change ends so both teams got equal advantage.

Everyone who came to MacKenzie's lot got to play. We sometimes had fifteen on a side. In those games a bad fake going through the line meant being crushed under a mountain of bodies or dragged mercilessly over the rocks and ruts back to your goal line. But most of the time the teams numbered eight or nine players and the games were fast and rough.

It was three weeks to the day of our night rafting adventure: a beautiful October morning, the air crisp and clear, a scattering of brown leaves covering the damp ground. Mickey Harrington and Fritz Beamer had chosen up teams. I was on Fritz's team along with Weed, Tony DeVito, Tim Scooty, Butch Kucher, Bobby Wade, and Matt Litsky. Mickey had Buzzy, Scuff, Amos, Fats, Joe Sweeney, Johnny Beers, and Bebe Dunker. The teams were evenly matched, but Mickey was a fast runner and hard to bring down. I hated playing defense against him. He'd tuck his head and drive into you like a cannonball. Fritz liked to pass. Since I was playing left end on his team that meant lots of pass plays on offense and stopping Mickey's tough end runs on defense.

Amos flipped a coin and Fritz called it. Our team got to receive. Mickey chose to defend the scotch pines, so our team lined up on the sidewalk by the road. A few yards out from the pines Fats kicked up a small mound of dirt with the back of his sneaker. Then he placed the football upright in the mound. Mickey came over, put his arm on Fat's shoulder, and whispered something in his ear. I figured he was telling him to kick it over toward Matt and Bobby. He didn't want Fritz to get it. We had a rule that if you got the ball on the kick-off and didn't move, you could pass it. It was one of Fritz's favorite plays. He'd get the ball, look like he was deciding which way to run and lob a quick pass over the charging defense. Fats gave an understanding nod and took a few steps backward.

"Ready?" he yelled.

"Ready!" we yelled back.

He charged the football and kicked it low and hard. It spiraled to about mid-field, hit and bounded high into the air spinning. As it came down Bobby tried to catch it, but the ball bounced through his hands. He turned to chase after it, but Tony came by and gave him a shove: "Leave it alone! Get blocking!" he yelled.

The ball bounced erratically back toward the sidewalk. Tony scooped it up and ran. Weed and I crowded in front of him blocking out Amos, Scuff, and Johnny Beers. But Buzzy hooked in from the side and drove into Tony's legs. As Tony was going down he handed off to Fritz. Fritz faked out Joe Sweeney and managed a couple of extra yards before Mickey and Fats brought him down.

Our first game of the season was on. As the morning progressed, groups of townspeople gathered to watch for a while and then went on their way. Occasionally a truck or car would pull up across the street and toot the horn when we scored. Up and down MacKenzie's lot we scrambled— passing, blocking, and tackling. It was great fun, but by eleven o'clock I was wiped out. I'd run about ten miles of pass plays and collided with Mickey at least twenty times. Mick's toughest play was the "statue of liberty." Amos would quarterback the ball up close to the hiker, then fade back to pass. As he brought his arm back to throw, Mick would come around behind him, snatch the ball from his hand, and charge full speed into the line. That really wiped me out. But I couldn't quit. If you were a little kid you could quit and nobody noticed, but I was one of the biggest and oldest boys on the field and that meant playing until everyone dropped or the noon whistle blew.

"Listen up!" Fritz said as we gathered in a huddle. "We're one touchdown behind and it's third down. We've got to go for a long one. John, you and Weed head for the street but cross just before the sidewalk. Tony, go straight out to where Bebe's standing and turn. I'll hit you if I get in trouble. Scooty, you and Matt fall back and block. Butch, Tim, Bobby, you slow down Amos and Mickey at the line. Get in front of them. Don't be scared. Hike on four."

116

"Can I hike this time?" Butch asked.

Butch was a sixth grader.

"Okay," Fritz said, "but get it back in the air. Don't screw up!"

Butch nodded, strutted fearlessly up to the line and straddled the ball. Fats and Joe Sweeney stood across the scrimmage line smiling at him. He bent over and clutched the ball with both hands.

"Reaaaady," Fritz called out making sure we were in position, "hut one! hut two! hut...."

Uffff! Crunch!

Before Butch even hiked the ball Fats and Joe lunged over the line knocking him into a heap. Fats lay on the ground hugging the football.

"Our ball! Our ball!" Scuff, Amos, Buzzy, and Joe yelled.

"What's going on," Fritz shouted flailing his arms in the air, "have you guys gone nuts? He didn't even hike it!"

"He lifted the ball off the ground," Joe said getting up. "Fats and I saw it."

Butch shook his head. "No, I didn't! I never lifted the ball off the ground!"

117

"You calling us liars?" Joe said giving Butch a push backward.

Weed walked up to Joe and grabbed him by the shirt. "I'll call you a liar. You and Fats were planning to dump Butch before the play even started. I heard you talking!"

Joe and Fats burst into laughter, Fats rolling on the ground.

"Come on you jerks! You're messing up the game," Tony grumbled.

"Oh dear! Messing up the game," Fats mocked.

Tony's face flashed red with anger. He had a quick temper. He dove on Fats, trying to grab the ball away, but Fats tossed it to Mickey. Tony then grabbed Fats around the neck. Fats rolled over on top of him. Tony struggled to push Fats off but couldn't move him.

"Get off or I'll slug you," Tony threatened.

Fats smiled and rolled off.

"We're taking a five yard penalty," Fritz announced as the two boys got up.

"Five yards, my aunt Fanny!" Mickey shouted. "Take the down over."

I had slumped under a large maple tree at the side of the field and was enjoying the break. Buzzy came over and joined me.

"Too nice a day for football," he said. "Let's go exploring or something."

"Fritz's getting real mad," I said. "If he and Mick get into a fight, the game's over."

Fritz glared at Mickey. "Five yards," he repeated.

"Stuff it, Beamer," Mickey said.

"Gimme the ball," Fritz demanded.

Mickey threw the ball on the ground. It bounced across the field. Fritz rushed at him, and the two boys locked arms. They danced in a circle kicking with their feet trying to throw each other down. Amos hurried over and tried to break them apart. The three staggered about and fell into the dirt sending up a cloud of dust. Mickey and Fritz were quick to their feet, but Amos was already up and between them.

"We're supposed to be playing football," he shouted. "If you guys want to fight, wait'll the game's over."

The two boys stared at each other threateningly.

"What about the penalty?" Fritz said.

"Make it one yard with the down over," Amos replied.

They looked at Mickey. Mickey hesitated and then nodded.

"Good old Amos saves the day," Buzzy said, yawning. "Too bad. Mickey would have killed Beamer."

The New Girl

The two of us got up from the tree and sauntered back on the field. Amos stepped off the penalty and put the ball down.

"Huddle," Fritz yelled and we gathered in a circle a few feet from the ball. "Same play on two: John and Weed long, Tony look for the quickie. Scoot, hike the ball. See if you can trip up Fats. You little kids block."

Back to the scrimmage line we went and took our positions.

"I've got John," Mickey yelled, "Scuff, you take Weed; Buzzy, stay with Tony."

As Scooty bent over the ball I noticed three girls coming down the sidewalk pushing a baby carriage. One girl was Kate Darby and the other Jeanne Page, both in the seventh grade. The third girl I'd never seen before but she was very pretty. The carriage looked like something out of a museum. It was woven of brown wicker, had four enormous spoked wheels, and the polished brass metalwork. The girls were chatting as they approached the edge of the lot. They didn't even seem to notice the football game.

'Reaaady!" Fritz called. "Hut one! Hut two!"

Scooty snapped the ball back and I took off down the field. Mickey was staying close. About five yards from the sidewalk I faked left and broke across the field. I couldn't believe it. The three girls with the baby carriage were strolling right into the play. I'd gained a couple of steps on Mickey so Fritz let loose with a long, spiraling pass. It arched beautifully over the field, but when it peaked and started down I knew it was too high. I ran another step and leapt as high as I could with my arm extended in the air. The ball just grazed my fingers, wobbled slightly, and headed right for the baby carriage. It slammed into the front wheel where it stuck in the spokes. The carriage skidded to a stop. The three girls looked at each other in surprise and horror. Kate quickly ran around to the side of the carriage. Seeing the football stuck in the spokes she gave a little cry.

"You've ruined Mrs. Crawford's carriage! Just look at it! It's an antique! It's over one hundred years old!"

From inside the carriage came a faint wail. Jeanne reached in and lifted out what looked like a bundle of laundry. The wail was coming from inside.

"You've made the baby cry," she said. "You could have injured him. He's very upset."

My friends and I stood frozen on the field. We didn't have the faintest idea how to deal with the situation.

Kate spun around from the carriage, clenched both her fists, and placed them on her hips. She was a short, attractive girl with dark skin, dark hair, and intense brown eyes.

"You boys and your silly, stupid football. This is a public walk, not Yankee Stadium. Every Saturday morning you're out here terrifying old ladies and stopping traffic. Now you've made this little baby cry and broken its carriage."

There was a long silence. "Maybe we can fix the wheel," Mickey finally spoke. He looked at me and motioned with his head. The two of us walked over to the carriage and knelt by the wheel. The others crowded around to watch.

"I'll hold the wheel," I said. "You get the football out."

I took hold of the wheel. Mickey gripped the football. He carefully twisted and turned it until it popped loose from the spokes. The football was fine but at least five spokes were bent.

"I'm going to need pliers," I said sitting back on the sidewalk.

"I've got a pair in the garage—back in a sec," Mickey responded. He jumped up, tossed the football to Fritz, and took off up the field. At the end of the lot he disappeared into the pines. Mickey's house was next to the church. His father was the minister. A few seconds later he burst back through the pines carrying the pliers. He ran up and handed them to me.

I took the pliers and began pushing and pulling on the bent spokes. Kate and Jeanne remained on the sidewalk playing with the baby, but the new girl came over and gently dropped to her knees in the grass next to me.

"It's nice of you to fix the wheel," she said. "The carriage belongs to my aunt. The baby's my cousin."

Behind me I could hear Weed and Scuff coughing as if they had something stuck in their throats. I felt my face redden and tried to turn away so the girl wouldn't see. 'I'll kill those two when I get done,' I thought to myself.

"Do you fix things a lot?" she asked.

"Yeah, I guess so," I replied. "My grandfather's got a barn full of tools. He used to farm. He's taught me a lot."

"Conversation's getting heavy," I heard Weed whisper loudly to Scuff, "John's grandfather has a whole barn full of tools."

"Wow, that's something," Scuff exclaimed. I tried as best I could to ignore them. The girl didn't seem to notice.

"Do you live in Delhi—in the town?" she continued.

I nodded. "On Elm Street. It's the next street over, along the river."

"My aunt lives on Sheldon Drive up by the school: the green and white house with the big porch across the front. Her husband is Judge Crawford."

"My father knows Judge Crawford. He sometimes goes down to the court house to see him—usually when col-

122

lege students get in trouble. Last year some guys from a fraternity got caught unbolting a mortar from the soldiers' monument. Your uncle made them scrub down the whole monument with toothbrushes.It took them an entire Saturday."

The spokes were almost straightened. I wanted to ask the girl where she came from and how long she'd be visiting, but I was too embarrassed with all my friends standing around.

"Okay," I said, "that's the best I can do. One of the spokes is broken. It'll have to be welded. Stop by Ridley's Garage next to the Western Auto and ask for Okie. Tell him we broke it. He'll fix it for free."

At a glance you couldn't tell the wheel had been damaged. Kate and Jeanne hurried over. They looked at the wheel and were delighted. The new girl smiled and said her aunt would take care of the broken spoke. It was the first time I had looked at her up close. She was as pretty as Christina Wetzel but very different. Her hair was black and wavy and her eyes light green. She had a round face that seemed to brighten when she spoke, and a single dimple that appeared when she smiled. She wasn't at all shy. I liked her a lot and probably would have sat there staring at her all afternoon if Amos hadn't interrupted.

"Throw the ball, Fritz," he shouted, starting up the field. "Take the down over."

"Naw," Fritz said, kicking a clump of loose grass, "I don't feel like playing anymore."

Amos stopped so suddenly he almost tripped over his own feet. He turned and looked at Fritz with disbelief. Fritz, Joe, and Tony were standing with Kate and Jeanne. They'd walked around while I was working on the wheel. I heard Tony invite them to his father's store for sodas.

"I'm quitting too," Tony said. "I've got other things to do."

"Me too," Joe nodded.

The girls put the baby back into the carriage and started down the street.

"We've still got almost an hour till noon!" Amos protested.

The three boys ignored him and hurried after the girls. When they'd caught up the new girl asked if we were coming too.

"They want to keep playing football," Fritz told her.

"But you've got the football," she said.

The three boys laughed. "Looks like they'll have to find their own football," Joe scoffed.

"You're a jerk, Sweeney," Scuff shouted after them.

We stood watching until they'd crossed the street by the Ford Garage.

"Let's follow them and mess up the party," Fats suggested.

"Yeah," Weed grinned, "I'd like to see Beamer drink a soda with a football stuck in his mouth."

"Forget it," Mickey said. "Tony's father'll throw us out. Robbie Barns got thrown out a month ago just for climbing over a booth, and he still can't go in."

"Anyone got a football?" Amos asked.

We all shook our heads.

"I can't believe those girls came right on the field during a play," Mickey grumbled.

"Yeah, real dumb," Fats agreed.

"Who's the new girl?" Buzzy asked.

Mickey shrugged his shoulders. "Don't know. She sure is pretty. I've never seen a girl with green eyes like hers."

"She likes John," Butch said meekly.

"Shut up, Kucher," Weed yelled, grabbing him around the neck. "If we want to hear from you little kids we'll squeeze your heads."

He rubbed the top of Butch's head with his fist until Butch howled and threw him over backward on the ground.

"Yeah, you wimps don't know nothing about women," Scuff laughed. "The girl doesn't like John, she likes broken wheels. She probably hangs out in gas stations on weekends."

"You're real funny, Scuff," I said, slowly easing toward him. "You and Weed should be on stage—the ding-dong brothers."

As he and Weed laughed at each other, I grabbed Scuff's arm and slammed my fist into it just above the elbow.

"Oowww!" he yelled pulling back. "That hurt, man. That really hurt. Jeez, what'd you do that for?"

"That's for when I was working on the wheel. You're next, Weed."

Weed started dancing backward up the field. "You ain't going to dead-arm me," he yelled.

"Let's quit goofing around and do something," Buzzy said, "I'm getting bored."

"Yeah, me too," Fats agreed. "Standing around here ain't no fun."

"How about exploring the old burlap mill at the end of the railroad yard," Mickey suggested. "We've never been in there. I've heard it's filled with machinery and stuff. Maybe get some souvenirs for the tree house."

"It's all boarded up," Amos objected.

"Who cares," Scuff shrugged, "we'll find a way in."

Mickey turned to me. "What do you say, John?"

"Sounds great," I said.

"Let's get going!" Buzzy shouted. "The day's a-wasting."

Matt Litsky stepped forward. "Can me, Butch, Johnny, Bobby, and Bebe come too?"

"No!" Scuff said. He was still rubbing his arm. "We don't want any little kids tagging along. Exploring is serious business."

"You guys'll have to get lost," Mickey said. "You'd just get in the way."

The boys were disappointed but walked away. They knew better than to try and follow us.

"See you guys," Tim Scooty said starting up Clinton Street.

"Where you going, Tim?" Amos asked. "Come on with us."

"Yeah, come exploring with us," Fats joined in.

Tim turned his head but kept walking. "I'm going to watch cartoons. My grandmother's got a T.V. set. She lets me watch it on weekends."

Amos shook his head. "What fun is it to sit around all day looking at some dumb little box? You can't even see the picture. It's just a lot of fuzzy spots and scraggly lines."

Tim shrugged and continued down the street.

"You're a waste," Weed called after him.

"Forget Scooty," Buzzy said. "Come on, we've got some exploring to do."

126

Shortcut

We all felt pretty excited as we started up Main Street toward the railroad yard. It was always fun to explore old buildings around town. But we hadn't gotten far when Mickey stepped out in front of us and turned around.

"Wait up," he said holding up his hands. "I've got a great idea. Listen! Dud Morrison told me there's a 1932 Chevy pickup truck for sale at Miller's Feed Mill. Only thirty bucks. Let's take a look at it—it's on the way. Maybe we can buy it."

"What are we going to do with a pickup truck?" Scuff asked.

"Run it on the right-of-way where the tracks are torn up," I said.

"Yeah," Weed's eyes lit up, "or maybe run it on the back roads. I'll bet we can get to Hamden or Franklin or maybe even Walton on the back roads.

"I know plenty of girls in Walton!" Buzzy burst in. "We can take them for a picnic and swimming at Wilder's pond up Cat Hollow."

"Are you guys serious?" Amos asked.

"Maybe," Mickey said, "it can't hurt to take a look at the truck."

"Miller's Feed Mill's at the opposite end of the railroad yard from the old Burlap Mill," Fats said. "That ain't exactly on the way."'

"I know a shortcut," I said. "We cut through Burdee's backyard to Elm Street, then head down behind the John Deere Garage to Steele Creek. Once we cross the creek there's an old road through the brush. It ends right behind Miller's. From Miller's we walk the tracks to the Burlap Mill."

"Sounds good," Mickey slapped me on the back. Then he turned to Fats. "What do you say, Fats? You got enough horsepower to get to Steele Creek?"

"It'd better be a shortcut, that's what I say. I don't feel like walking all over the railroad yard."

"You'll see," I said.

Instead of continuing up Main Street we crossed to the other side and jogged back toward the center of town. After passing four houses, we came to the Burdee house. Like most of the houses along Main Street, the Burdee house was stately and well kept. It was a local landmark because of the great ornamented turret that rose almost three stories on one side. From a distance it looked like a castle. On top of the turret was a small porch. The porch was the greatest lookout in town. When I was a little kid the Burdees let my sister Kaye and me sit up there to watch a fireman's parade. We could see the bands and engines all the way up Main Street. For years after that I hoped my parents would buy the house just so I could sit up on the turret. Behind the Burdee house lay a large green lawn filled with carefully tended flower beds and surrounded by a tall cedar board fence. Cautiously we entered the backyard from the driveway, first making sure Mr. Bly, the gardener, wasn't around, then zig-zagged our way through the flower beds to the rear fence. There we pulled up a loose board behind a juniper shrub, and one by one squeezed through into a narrow alley between two barns. The alley felt cool and damp and smelled of a dead animal.

"Let's get out of here fast," Fats cried covering his face with his arm, "this place smells worse than a week-old diaper pail."

Fats knew what diaper pails were all about. He had a brand-new month-old sister.

Scuff was just in front of me. "Look there," he said pointing a few feet ahead. Lying half under one barn was the bloated body of a brown rat with flies buzzing all around it.

"Remember how Huck Finn and Tom Sawyer used a

dead rat to cure warts," Amos said. "I wonder if it really worked?"

"That was a dead cat," Mickey grumbled.

"Whatever it was this one's all yours, Muss," Scuff laughed. "Let me know how you make out."

"Keep going," I said giving him a shove. "There's a door at the end."

The eight of us hurried past the dead animal holding our noses, exited a rickety door covered with bugs and cobwebs, and emerged on Elm Street between the Gilly greenhouses and Marlow backyard. Across the street was the John Deere garage.

"Pretty good shortcut—yeah?" I beamed.

"Yeah, great," Mickey nodded, "how'd you ever find it?"

"Burdee boys use it all the time. I saw them coming past my house to school every morning and figured they had a shortcut. I followed them home one day."

"Where to now?" Amos asked.

"Steele Creek behind the John Deere garage," Buzzy said."Come on!"

We ran across the street and down a dirt road cluttered with tractors and farm machinery. The road passed a tall, dingy, cinder block garage, and ended in a junkyard filled with discarded parts. Bearing right, we followed a row of oil drums and shortly came to where the yard dropped off sharply into Steele Creek. There a narrow plank bridge crossed the stream. It was supported in the middle by an ancient tractor half-submerged in the water.

Before the rest of us had reached the stream, Weed broke away, raced up the planks, and stood facing us on the tractor. He began beating on his chest and shouting, "Me Tarzan!"

Scuff tried to follow, but Weed jumped up and down on the planks until Scuff slipped and fell into the water.

"You're stupid, Weed, really stupid," Scuff cried as he fought the current to stand up. His teeth were clenched and his face beet red.

Weed roared with laughter. "Poor Scuffy fell down. Got his pants all wet," he mocked.

"Let's get him," Mickey whispered to Amos.

The two boys ran out on the planks. Mickey got to within a couple of feet of Weed with Amos right behind him. Weed didn't have time to rock the boards but he had the advantage of standing on the tractor. He suddenly lunged forward pushing Mickey into Amos. The two boys lost their footing on the flimsy boards and toppled into the stream.

Weed was delighted. He did a little victory dance on the tractor and then shouted, "Who's next?"

"Come on, Barn," Fats yelled, "we're supposed to be exploring not klutzing around in the stream."

"Ooooh! fatsy, watsy—maybe you'd like to try crossing next," Weed taunted. "Come on, blimpo, I'm waiting."

Fats shook his head and looked disgusted. "This is just like the time you wouldn't stop throwing acorns at Smith's bull. We all ended up getting chased into the swamp."

Mickey and Amos climbed up on the bank and began emptying their sneakers of sand and water. Scuff remained standing knee-deep in the stream looking as if he were trying to decide whether or not to continue across. Meanwhile Buzzy had been poking around in the bushes and returned carrying a long stick. He broke off the ends until the weight felt comfortable.

"Wow!" Weed exclaimed as he relaxed against the tractor, "Buzzy found himself a big stick to play with. I'm impressed."

Buzzy didn't say anything but started slowly out over the water. Weed waited until he was halfway to the tractor and then began bouncing furiously on the planks. Buzzy held the stick out, just managing to keep his balance while inching forward. Seeing he couldn't bounce him off, Weed reached down to lift one of the boards; but Buzzy quickly slammed the thick end of the stick into his shin. Weed howled with pain and began jumping up and down holding the shin.

"You didn't have to bust my leg," he cried.

Scuff had been circling closer to the tractor. Now he saw his chance. He jumped up on the wheel, grabbed Weed by the back of the shirt and pulled him over backward into the stream. Weed made a huge splash as he hit. He was soaked from head to foot, but still managed a rowdy laugh as he surfaced through the foam.

As Weed and Scuff sloshed on across the stream, Buzzy, Fats, and I took the bridge. We gathered on the other side to look over the area. Although we could see one of Miller's yellow grain elevators through the trees, there lay a good hundred feet of thick brush and brambles between us and the mill fence.

"This ain't going to be no cake-walk," Amos said kicking into a tangled mat of vines and thorns. "This place is a regular jungle."

"Spread out," I said. "Look for an opening."

131

We spread out along the bank and began poking into the brush. Amos was right; it was the biggest briar patch I'd ever seen. Blackberry, thornbush and wild rose were interwoven with wild grape and ivy. Along the edge grew thick clumps of purple loosestrife and mustard.

"We should have stuck to Main Street," Fats complained, "we ain't never going to get through this mess."

"Keep looking," I said. "The old road's in there somewhere."

"Old road, my foot," Weed yelled from under a blanket of leaves, "the last thing that came through here either flew or crawled on its belly."

Mickey shook his head. "Fats is right. Even with cutters and gloves it'd take us all morning to get to the fence."

Just then Scuff charged out from between two bushes flailing his hands about his head. Tiny yellow dots were dancing and buzzing around him. He slid down the stream bank and began throwing water into the air.

"Great shortcut, John," he howled, "three acres of brambles, yellow jackets and probably quicksand too."

I was beginning to doubt we would ever find the path. It had been a couple of years since I'd last seen the road. The creek had wandered washing away old landmarks, and the vegetation grown dense. If we didn't find the road, we'd have to follow the stream back toward Elm Street until we found a break in the brush.

"Hey, John, come here!" Buzzy called from downstream. "Think I found the road!"

The rest of us hurried along the bank to where Buzzy was standing by a large fallen oak tree.

"Look in under here," he said. He bent down and disappeared into a small opening under the trunk of the tree. I followed and immediately recognized the rocky gully as part of the old road.

"This is it!" I shouted to the others. "The tree covered up the road entrance."

"What an escape route," Buzzy exclaimed excitedly. "Someone's chasing you along the bank and—presto!— you dive under the trunk and vanish."

"Yeah," I said, "even if they found the opening, they wouldn't know where it went."

Mickey slid in behind us. "Let's get going," he said, "I want to see that '32 Chevy pickup."

Miller's Feed Mill

We started crawling along the gully, keeping low to avoid the tangle of thorns and vines overhead. It was like going through a tunnel. I was more worried about snakes than the overgrowth. There'd been rumors of rattlesnakes around the railroad yard. I'd read that they liked dry, rocky places. I'd also read that if you moved slowly and gave them plenty of warning they'd clear out, but if you surprised them, they'd strike. Grandpa had once seen a dead rattlesnake down below Walton on route 10. It'd gotten run over by a truck. It was almost six feet long and as big around as a man's arm. Grandpa said that one good bite from a snake like that could kill a boy quick. Since I was in the lead going up the gully, I decided to throw rocks ahead of me to scare anything off. Buzzy thought it was pretty funny throwing rocks up a gully. While we were resting he stuck a stick up my pant leg and half scared the wits out of me. But a little further on we came across a snakeskin on the rocks that was easily a yard long. After that he didn't fool around any more.

Fortunately we didn't meet with anything worse than an orange salamander and a couple of furry spiders. When the brambles ended we were able to walk and quickly made our way to the chain-link fence surrounding the mill. The mill was a long, two-story, clapboard building with a raised loading dock for trucks and four double-door entrances. Two giant grain elevators rose up through the roof. Tracks extended beyond the far side, and the end of a rusty boxcar was visible at the back corner. Between the fence and building lay a large dirt parking lot. It was badly rutted from trucks and pocked with numerous puddles of black, oily water. The only entrance to the lot was through a narrow open gate at the front. There was another gate for the railroad cars, but it was padlocked.

"There's the truck!" Mickey yelled pointing to the side of a barn behind the main building. "Ain't she a beaut?"

The rest of us looked and beheld an ancient, faded-gray pickup with dented fenders, broken windows, four flat tires, and no bumpers parked at the side of the garage. A hand written 'FOR SALE' sign was held to the windshield by a bent wiper.

Scuff began banging his head against the chain-link fence. "I got soaked in the stream, stung by yellow jackets and torn up by brambles just to see that pile of junk!"

135

"Cut it out," Mickey said giving him a punch. "Wait'll you see it up close."

"Hey, how come the place is so deserted?" Amos asked.

"The men must be on break," I said. "Let's get over the fence before they get back."

We scrambled up the fence, swung carefully over the barbed wire top and dropped into the yard. Only Fats got hung up on the barbed wire. Buzzy had to climb back up and unhook his pants. Once we were all on the ground we raced for the truck, Mickey in the lead. As soon as we got to it he began kicking the tires and bouncing up and down on the fenders.

"I told you it was a beaut," he shouted. "We'll strip off the hood, paint the engine silver, the body bright red and add an exhaust cutout for extra noise."

"Let's see if we can start her up," Weed said, opening the driver's door and jumping in. Mickey climbed in on the other side. Together the boys began twisting and pulling knobs on the dashboard and jerking the floor shift around.

"You two are crazy!" Amos exclaimed, backing away from the truck. "You start it up and we'll get our butts kicked all over this lot!"

"Rooom! Rooom!" Weed hollered and spun the wheel recklessly.

"They ain't never going to get it started unless one of them gets out and cranks the engine," Buzzy spoke to Amos under his breath.

"You sure about that?" Amos wondered.

"Yeah, this thing's ancient. Built in the early thirties. I once saw one like it at my uncle's garage."

After a while Weed and Mickey got bored and climbed out. Buzzy and I got in and looked it over.

"What do you think?" Mickey said, leaning in the window.

"Thirty bucks is cheap," I said. "If we each put in five, we'll have enough left over for a couple tanks of gas."

"Let's find out who owns it and see if it really runs," Buzzy suggested.

"Yeah, come on, we'll ask up at the office," Weed said, "we'll tell them we want to see it run." He was already moving toward the building.

Buzzy and I jumped out. The seven of us hurried across the graveled lot and along the loading dock toward the front office.

"Are we really going to buy it?" Fats muttered.

"Yeah, if it runs," I said.

"Where are we going to keep it?" Scuff asked.

"Down here someplace...or maybe even in my backyard."

We'd just passed the loading dock when Weed, Mickey, and Amos, who were in front, stopped so abruptly the rest of us stumbled into them. Before we could say a word Mickey turned and whispered, "Shhhh! Look outside the gate!"

The Truckers

I looked up beyond the office. Less than a hundred feet away strolling past the entrance gate was the entire Trucker gang. They were talking and throwing around a small rubber ball. Bertie Grimes was carrying an armful of fishing poles. They'd been down behind the old Jeffery creamery fishing. We stood frozen by the building. So far they hadn't seen us. Then Billy "Bones" Lord whipped the ball over to Bull Fano. It glanced off Bull's fingers and banged into the fence where it stuck. Bull walked over to pull it out and looked right at us. His face lit up with a strange, malicious grin. He placed his hands on his hips and called: "Hey, brothers, we've got company. Look who's here."

The other members stopped and wandered back to the fence. They too began to smile.

"Didn't your moms tell you not to play in the railroad yard," Roy Scutter said, leaning against a post. "You kiddies are in big trouble."

"Yeah, like rats caught in a cage," his brother, Luke, snickered.

Jake Bonner rattled the fence. "Ain't nobody going to help you down here," he said.

Billy Bones ambled over to Turk McGraw and put his arm over Turk's shoulder. "Isn't that your little pal fuzzy-wuzzy—the one that's been causing all the trouble?"

McGraw squinted his eyes and nodded.

"We'll dip him in the tar pit, eh, Turk?"

"First I'm going to have some punching practice," Turk muttered, "then the tar pit."

Gideon Spicky glanced over at Roy. "Enough talk, Scut?"

Roy spit into the dirt. "Yeah," he nodded, "enough talk."

"Just make sure Hoffman or Fancher don't get away," Turk warned.

"Let's get 'um!" Luke shouted.

A yell went up from the Truckers that sent cold chills down my back. Their sneakers kicked up dust and gravel as they rounded the gate and spilled into the mill yard. Gideon and Bones were in the lead.

"Let's go for the fence," Mickey said.

"Too late," I cried grabbing his arm. "They'll pull us down. Try and lose them in the mill."

We raced to the loading dock, climbed up and stumbled through the nearest door. Inside was a huge storage room with a ceiling almost twelve feet high. About the room islands of feed bags were stacked pyramid fashion. We snaked our way through the islands until we came to a large pyramid of red and green bags near the back wall. Since there were no open doors along the wall, our only chance of escaping the Truckers was to climb the pyramid and hide on top. We scrambled up the steep sides clutching at the burlap and wedging our toes between bags. The top was flat with about a foot clearance to the ceiling. The air near the ceiling was hot and dusty and smelled of molasses. We pulled ourselves over the edge and lay motionless trying to still our breathing.

Suddenly voices and running footsteps echoed throughout the room. I cautiously lifted my head and peered over the top. There was a Trucker standing in every door while others searched among the feed piles. Outside I could see Gideon watching the front to make sure we didn't escape through the office. The Truckers searched for a long time. Three of four walked by the pyramid on top of which we were hiding.

"They've got to be in here somewhere," I hear Luke grumble.

"What about the office?" Jake said.

"Bertie looked in the windows. They ain't in there," Bull replied.

"Well, they just didn't disappear!" Turk roared.

"There's one place we didn't look," Roy drawled slowly. He stood silently gazing about the room. The mill suddenly seemed as quiet as a morgue. Butterflies began to chase through my stomach.

"Yeah, Roy," his brother coaxed.

"Up on top of the feed piles—that's where!"

"Yeah, up on top of the feed piles," Luke repeated slowly.

"Spread out! Each take a pile!" Jake commanded.

A wave of cold fear swept over me. Like Roy had said— we were in big trouble. It'd mean a fight when they found us and we'd get the worst of it. I dropped my face into the feed bags. The sweet smell almost made me sick.

Buzzy was lying next to me. He nudged me and whispered, "They're going to find us for sure but we'll put up a good fight."

"Yeah," I muttered.

"John, Buzzy, take the left side," Mickey whispered. "Fats, you and Muss take the front. Weed and I'll take the right side. Scuff watch the back. If you need help yell. We'll hold them off as long as we can."

Footsteps approached and I felt someone climbing the pile. Then Buzzy gave a cry, and began to squirm and kick. I looked over his back and saw Jake Bonner's grinning face. He had Buzzy by the leg and was trying to pull him down. Weed saw him too. He swung over and pushed a feed bag into his chest. Jake tried to hang on but the weight was too much and he crashed to the floor with the bag. The other Truckers came running over to see what had happened.

"Get this feed bag off me," Jake groaned.

Bull and Luke pulled away the bag.

"They're all up on top of here," he said getting up.

Luke immediately started up our side. When he got almost to the top, Buzzy and I pushed off a bag and sent him tumbling down again.

"Surround the pile," Roy ordered, "we'll all go up together."

The Truckers surrounded the pyramid. As soon as they started up we began dumping off bags. We knocked them all down at first, but it was a temporary victory. Bones, Bull, and Turk ganged up and attacked Weed and Mickey's side. Weed pushed Bull off, and Mickey toppled Turk, but Bones got between them and crawled up on top into the middle of us. He was swinging his fist as hard as he could. It was like meeting a wildcat under a barn. Mickey finally got his arms around Bones and Buzzy gave him a punch in the stomach knocking the wind out of him. Then Weed and Fats dumped him off. But no sooner was Bones down than Gideon got between Amos and me. Gideon was pure muscle. He doubled up Amos with a poke to the ribs and then he went for me. I managed to grab one of his fists but he hit me square in the jaw with the other. I fell back dazed. Stars seemed to fill the whole mill. Fats dove at Gideon, got him around the legs, and with one big shove pushed him head first off the pile. Gideon tumbled to the floor.

As the Truckers prepared for another assault a gruff voice suddenly roared across the store room: "What are you kids doing? Why are you knocking all them feed bags down for? Dutch! Pete! Shorty! Get in here and see what these damn kid's done!"

It was the mill foreman Mike Macpherson. The Truckers didn't wait for Dutch, Pete, and Shorty. They took off though the room in every direction. The big foreman ran down Luke and hurled him through an open door. Luke skidded across the dock and disappeared over the edge in a cloud of dust. The other men caught Jake and Bones on the dock and sent them sprawling into the gravel below.

"Don't let me catch you boys in here again or I'll ...," Macpherson raised a clenched fist and shook it in the air.

We crawled to the center of the pyramid and lay as flat as possible.

"Must be they didn't see us," Amos said.

"We'll get the same treatment as the Truckers when they do," Scuff warned.

"Shhh! They're coming back. Keep down," Buzzy said.

The men returned to the pyramid and stood talking in low voices.

"One bag busted."

"Yeah, and twenty scattered about."

"Dumb kids fooling around. Mr. Miller seen this and he'd have the police on them."

"We don't need no police. They come in here again and we'll bust some heads."

"Shorty, get the loader. Clean this mess up. Dutch, you and Pete finish that third stack."

The men walked away.

Fats turned to me with a worried look. "We'd better get out of here fast," he said.

"Mick, Buzz, and I will scout the mill. Rest of you stay low," I said.

We crawled up to the front edge and looked around. Pete and Dutch were only about twenty away, stacking bags.

"We'll have to climb down the back and make a run for it," I whispered.

142

Buzzy tapped me on the arm and pointed to one of the open doors. "Look outside," he said.

I looked out across the yard. Just visible were the sneakers and pants of three Truckers. They were resting against the chain-link fence. Through another door I could see Roy and Turk back near the truck.

I nudged Mickey. "The Truckers are waiting for us outside. They've got the whole side of the building covered."

"Yeah, I see them," Mickey nodded. "They're staying near the fence in case the workmen come out."

The three of us crawled back to the center.

"The Truckers have the place surrounded," Mickey told the others. "Even if we get past the workmen we'd never make it to the gate. Our only chance is to avoid the workmen and maybe hide out till closing."

"We'll never hide in here till closing," Amos said. "They're moving all around this place. They'll find us for sure."

"You have any better ideas?" Mickey said.

Amos shook his head.

"Listen!" Buzzy cocked his ear, "the loader's on its way! We've got to get down!"

From somewhere near the office came the muffled putt-putt-putt of a small gasoline engine. We immediately started moving to the rear of the pyramid. At the edge Amos and I formed a sort of chain. He held my legs as I hung over the side on my stomach. One by one I helped ease the others down so as not to make any noise. Then Mickey and Weed caught Amos and me by the feet and lowered us to the floor. As I was sliding down I noticed a ladder bolted to a concrete pillar near the back wall. Once on the floor I crept over to the ladder and looked up. It ended at a trap door. If we could get to the second floor we might find a place to hide among the elevators. Cautiously I climbed the ladder. When I reached the top I was almost in a panic that the door would be locked. Out of the corner of my eye I could see the loader approaching from the front of the building. Putting one hand against the door, I slowly pushed. It creaked open sending a rain of dust and grain into my face. I pushed it further and stuck my head through. The upstairs was a big barn-like structure crisscrossed with metal ducts and wooden chutes. The only light came from four small, dirty windows along the walls. A giant electric motor rumbled and sparked a few feet away. In the ceiling pulleys driven by leather belts whirred. Everything was covered with dust. It gave the machinery a fuzzy appearance as if there'd been a snowstorm.

Holding the door open I ducked down and gave a little whistle to the others. Seeing me on the ladder they hurried over. One by one they started up. I climbed into the upper room and gave them a hand coming through the opening.

Amos and Scuff were the last two on the ladder. As Amos was climbing through the opening and Scuff waiting just below, the loader came around the side of the pyramid. Shorty spotted the boys. He jumped off the loader and began yelling. The two men stacking feed bags hurried over. One of them ran to the ladder and started up after Scuff. Mickey, Weed, Amos, and I grabbed Scuff by the arms, snatched him through the opening, and slammed the door shut.

"Find something heavy!" Amos yelled.

He and I stood on the door while the others rummaged about the room. We could feel the man pushing below. Weed and Fats soon returned, dragging bags of feed which we piled on the door.

"Scout the place!" I shouted.

We all took off in different directions.

"Hallway and stairs over here," Buzzy called from the front of the room, "probably go down to the office."

"Door and stairs back here," Mickey called from the opposite end.

Just then footsteps sounded on the rear stairs."They're coming up!" Scuff shrieked.

Amos and Scuff ran for the door and helped Mickey slide it shut.

"There's a lock," Mickey pointed in front of Scuff.

Scuff fumbled clumsily with the metal hasp and finally managed to snap it over the staple. "Quick! Someone find a bolt," he cried.

Fats ran over with a piece of wire which the two of them looped through the staple. The men arrived and began pushing and pounding on the door.

"What the hell is going on around here," I heard Mike yell from somewhere below. There were more footsteps and voices.

"Stay there, Dutch!" Mike commanded.

I knew Mike, Pete, and Shorty were heading for the office and front stairs. There was no door on the front stairs. We had to get out fast. I looked around and saw that our only chance for escape, other than going back through the trap door, was the windows. But if we went back downstairs, we'd be trapped for sure. Weed must have had the same thought. He was already working on one of the windows on the side of the building away from the Truckers. It was a double hung sash type with just enough room to climb through.

Boxcars

"Someone get a stick or something," Weed shouted, his face red from pushing on the window. "This thing's stuck!"

Mickey hurried over with a broken shovel handle. The rest of us crowded around. Together Mickey and Weed jammed the handle into the crack between the sash and sill. Then Mickey rested all his weight on the handle. The window groaned and gradually slid up.

Weed stuck his head out.

"What do you see?" Scuff asked anxiously.

"There's a boxcar below, but it's a good ten foot drop—if you hit the top. If you don't ...." Weed shook his head.

Buzzy and I pushed Weed aside and leaned out the window. Weeds was right. The boxcar was a good ten feet below the window and about a foot from the building. It would be a dangerous jump, but no worse than getting our heads busted by the workmen.

"I'll go first," Buzzy said lifting himself up onto the sill, "I'll give you guys a hand coming down."

"What about the Truckers?" Amos asked.

Buzzy looked to the right and left. "They must all be on

the other side." He climbed through the window, took a sitting position on the sill, then pushed hard against the building with his hands and feet. He landed in the middle of the narrow metal catwalk that ran along the top of the car.

I climbed up into the window, but pushed too hard and almost tumbled off the far side of the catwalk. Fortunately Buzzy caught me. One by one the others climbed into the window and jumped. When it came Fats' turn I could tell he was really scared sitting in the window. Then he jumped short. His feet just caught the top of the boxcar and he started to fall backward into the building. Amos, Buzzy, and I grabbed him. We practically tore off his shirt but we kept him from falling. Mickey was the last to jump. The workmen were already in the room as he climbed through the window. He didn't wait to seat himself on the sill but instead leapt headlong into the middle of us. We caught him in the air.

The boxcar was coupled to three other boxcars, one in the rear and two toward the front. The front cars ran along the building toward the gate. As soon as Mickey was on his feet, we ran along the catwalk, jumped to the second car, ran along the top of it, and jumped to the third car. At the far end of the third car we started single file down a ladder to the ground. Mickey, Amos, and Fats were still on the ladder when one of the workmen stuck his head out the window and began swearing at us. The commotion brought Bull and Gideon circling around the back of the building. They didn't trust the workmen and were staying close to the fence. Luckily Scuff was crouched by the tracks watching between the boxcars and building and saw them first. "Truckers coming!" he exclaimed in a whisper. Mickey, Amos, and Fats jumped from the ladder and we all dropped into the tall grass next to the tracks.

"Think they saw us?" Amos asked.

"They'd be hollering their heads off if they had," I said.

Mickey lifted his head and watched the two Truckers through the tips of the grass. "There goes our chance of getting to the fence and climbing over," he muttered.

The workman at the window pulled his head in and slammed the window shut.

"They're suspicious," I said. "Start moving along the building toward the gate—but keep low. If we can get to the front without being seen, we'll have a chance of outrunning them."

"Outrun them to where?" Scuff asked. "Roy, Bones and Spickey are plenty fast."

There was a brief silence, then Amos spoke. "Let's head for the big warehouse down the tracks—where they repair the engines. There's a huge storage room in the front with a ladder that goes all the way to the ceiling. At the top a door unhooks and you can climb right out on the roof. My dad used to work there. He showed me around. It's real dark in the storage room and the ladder's way in back along the wall. The Truckers'll never see it. Even if they did it's four stories straight up. They'd never dare climb it with us up on top."

"You want us to climb four stories on an open ladder?" Fat's mouth dropped and his eyes bulged in disbelief. "I already almost killed myself jumping to that boxcar."

"Maybe you'd like to stay here and play patty-cake with Turk McGraw," Weed quipped.

"Get moving," Mickey said giving Weed and Fats a shove. "Gideon and Bull are almost to the boxcars."

"We'll crawl up the tracks, then get as close to the building as possible," I said.

Buzzy and I were lying next to each other. We raised our heads together and just caught a glimpse of the two Truckers coming up the track bed behind the last car. Buzzy took the lead. He crawled under the boxcar, rolled over on his back and slid underneath the wheel axle. He rolled again and began crawling on his stomach up the bed toward the front of the building. The rest of us quickly followed.

When I crawled out from under the boxcar I found the track bed blazing hot. Overhead the sun was approaching noon in a cloudless sky. Heat rose in shimmering waves from the gray gravel and black cinders. I began to think about Molly Crumb's camp on Spring Lake. That's where Buzzy and I had spent the previous Saturday. It'd been great. Swimming, sailing, and a picnic. Molly was a shy, pudgy girl with big brown eyes, short dark hair that hung in curls, and a little round mouth that reminded me of a cherry lifesaver. She sat next to me all seventh grade, and I figured she liked me because every time I looked over at her she'd be looking at me and blinking her big brown eyes. Molly never spoke to me once the whole year, just blinked her eyes. Sometimes it made me a bit uneasy. Then toward the end of summer she invited me up to her parents' camp on Spring Lake. She and I went sailing together, and every time I'd bring the boat about she'd sort of bump into me and give a little apologetic sigh. As we were heading back to the dock in the late afternoon, a big gust came up. The boat heeled hard and I'm not sure whether Molly slid or jumped into my lap. Regardless, the two of us tumbled into the bottom of the boat. Molly had one arm around my neck and I had the distinct feeling she wasn't going to let go. Fortunately the main sheet jammed and the boat capsized. Even then it wasn't until we were two feet into the lake that she finally let go. The next time I visited I brought Buzzy with me. We could have gone again today but instead decided to play football. 'What a brilliant choice,' I thought to myself as I pulled clump of cocklebur from my pant leg. 'Even having Molly Crumb stalking me all day would have been a whole lot better than crawling through weeds and hot gravel waiting to get beat up by the town toughs.'

Toward the front of the building we slid down into the grass between the building and track bed. The grass was sparse but still afforded enough cover to keep out of sight of the two Truckers. We had only a short distance to go to the corner, when a window banged open overhead and a voice called out:

"Hey! What are you doing crawling around on your bellies like a bunch of snakes?"

We all stopped and looked up. A short, skinny man with dull gray eyes and a face full of ragged whiskers was leaning out a second floor window staring at us. I recognized him as Shorty, the workman on the loader.

"I'll bet those boys out front are after you—ain't they. That's why you knocked down them feed bags. You boys was on top. They had you trapped."

He seemed pleased he'd figured it all out. None of us spoke. We just lay low in the grass hoping Gideon and Bull hadn't heard him.

Shorty took a bite from a tobacco stick and gazed over toward the barrel factory as he chewed it. After a couple of dozen chews, he spit the brown wad down on us. Some of the juice splattered on my shirt and pants.

"That's for messing up them feed bags," he said.

Then he saw the two Truckers approaching the boxcars. A malicious grin brightened his surly face. Sticking two fingers in his mouth he gave a series of sharp whistles. As the boys peered from behind the boxcar, he motioned down toward us with his hand. I stuck my head up and watched Gideon and Bull. They were talking together and eyeing the building. Then Gideon's arm shot out and he pointed right at me.

"Run for the gate!" I yelled. "They've seen us!"

In an instant we were on our feet and running. Overhead Storty was pounding his fists against the building shouting, "Catch them! Catch them! Let's see a fight!"

Weed picked up a handful of gravel which he hurled at Shorty as he passed under the window. The gravel hit the building like a load of buckshot. Shorty leapt up and slammed his head into the sash. The window fell shut trapping his neck against the sill. He let loose with the worst string of four-letter words I'd ever heard. It'd have been an education just to sit and listen to him.

Gideon and Bull started after us, but Gideon turned back around the building to alert the others. That saved us. Gideon could have easily have caught up with Fats or Scuff. Then the rest of us would have had to turn back and help. But Bull was muscle-bound and slow.

We were almost to the gate before a shout went up from the other side of the building. A wave of Truckers charged across the gravel with Roy in the lead. Now the chase was really on.

Through the gate and across the road we ran, then

down an open stretch of four parallel tracks toward a tall, box-like building clad in silver corrugated metal. VAN-DUNK WAREHOUSE was printed in bright orange letters across the top. It was about the length of a football field to the warehouse. We had the advantage of a good lead and we were used to the rough terrain of the railroad yard. The Truckers were pretty much a street gang. But Roy, Gideon, and Bones were fast. If they began closing on us, we'd have to cut off toward the Walton Road, and try and lose them in the coal and gravel sheds. Then it would be every man for himself.

Whizzz! a rock sailed by my head, hit the ground and bounced along the tracks. I could hear other rocks falling behind me. I glanced around. Fats and Scuff were keeping up but Roy, Gideon, and Bones were gaining. The other Truckers had fallen back and were throwing rocks. Buzzy was just ahead of me.

"We'll beat them to warehouse!" I yelled.

"Yeah, but not by much," he nodded.

The Warehouse Roof

The VanDunk Warehouse was close now. There were sheds attached to the far end and back. Along one side a steep roof projected out over a truck loading dock. It was about twelve feet below the main roof. It might be possible to jump to the loading dock roof from the main roof if we got in trouble. From there we could work our way around the building to the lower shed roofs. That made me feel better. After the reception we got from the workmen at Miller's Feed Mill, I didn't like the idea of being stuck up on top of a four-story warehouse roof with only an open ladder to get down.

"Stay on the far tracks and head for the open doors," Amos shouted as we passed a group of switches.

Two sets of tracks entered the warehouse through two huge sliding doors. The doors were about a foot open. Inside it looked dark and deserted.

"What about the Truckers?" Scuff said. "They're going to see us going in."

"They'll see us but they'll never find us," Amos replied.

We skipped over a rail to the middle of the tracks and raced for the open doors. I figured Roy, Gideon, and Bones were less than fifty feet behind us. As I passed through the doors a barrage of rocks clattered against the corrugated metal. Inside it was dark and the air heavy with the smell of burning metal. The room was enormous. Giant pulleys and cables hung from overhead I-beams. Wheels, metal frames, air tanks, couples and other parts of trains were strewn along a wide concrete floor. At the far end of the room a man was kneeling over the carriage of a flatcar, a welding torch in one hand and a thick mask held to his face in the other. As he put the torch to the metal the whole end of the room lit up and streams of sparks flew into the air and bounced across the floor.

"This way," Amos spoke in a hushed voice. We followed him up a wooden ramp, then down a long, narrow corridor. Stained, crumbling cardboard boxes were piled up on both sides. At the end we entered a storeroom even larger than the train shop. Pallets of crated machine parts littered the floor. Colored metal drums were stacked along the walls. Most had FLAMMABLE printed on the side and a few had a skull and crossbones. Amos pointed to the far corner of the room. In the dim light of three overhead skylights I could see a skinny black ladder going up the wall. It was an open ladder and it went straight up four stories. It took my breath away.

Scuff was studying the ladder too. "Holy cow!" he muttered. "We're going to climb up that? I'd rather get beat-up by the Truckers."

"Let's just hide somewhere down here among the boxes," I suggested.

"I'm with John," Fats said. "There must be a hundred places to hide in here."

"Not after what happened at Miller's," Mickey shook his head, "either we go up on the roof or we find a quick way out of here."

"This place is deserted," Fats protested. "There isn't anyone around except that welder."

"Mickey's right," Buzzy spoke up. "The Truckers or somebody's going to find us hiding in here, and then we're going to be trapped again. And maybe this time we won't be so lucky."

"Yeah," Weed agreed, "Ed Lynch told me they let attack dogs loose when they close this place up—big German Shepherds. They'd find us fast."

"Shhh. Listen," I said. "Someone's coming."

Everyone was quiet. Shortly voices broke from the far end of the corridor.

"It's the Truckers," Buzzy whispered. "They're heading this way."

"Follow me," Amos said starting across the storeroom. There's an exit door near the ladder. We'll ditch them in the building."

We followed him through a maze of pathways that gradually wove to the far end of the building. There we found a metal door with a red EXIT sign taped to it. Amos hit the panic bar and pushed open the door on the run. He took one stride over the door sill and collided head-long into Luke Scutter. Luke stood a full foot over Amos, but Amos was solid. He hit Luke square in the chest sending him flying backwards to the ground. Bertie and Jake were standing a few feet away. They were so surprised they just stared at Luke sprawled in the dust. Amos slid to a stop, swung around and dove back

154

through the door with the rest of us. As he passed through, Buzzy and I pulled the door shut.

"They've got the place surrounded!" Scuff cried.

"Follow me," Amos said.

He raced along the wall to the ladder, leapt to about the fourth rung and within seconds had climbed the four stories to the top. There he crouched holding on by one arm and began scouting the storeroom. It made me dizzy just watching him. I wondered if it was his Indian blood that made him so fearless of heights.

"Come on!" he called to us.

Buzzy started up first, then Mickey, Fats, and Scuff. When it came my turn I didn't think I could do it. High places had always bothered me. Even as a child I'd liked to stay on the ground. One time my sister, Kaye, climbed out through the cupola onto the roof of my grandfather's two-story barn in Walton. She was five and I was four. I watched enviously from the garden as she scampered about the roof like a squirrel; but when she waved for me to come up, I dug my feet into the loose dirt of my grandmother's garden, crossed my arms and refused to budge. Looking up the ladder I felt like I was back in the garden again, but this time I had to go. Only Weed and I remained on the floor. All the others had gone up—even Fats. I couldn't "chicken out".

My heart was pounding, and my legs were all rubbery as I gripped the rungs and started up. "Don't look down. Don't look down," I repeated over and over to myself. Each step was a trial and it seemed like there were a thousand steps. I had to block out any thought of falling to the concrete floor below or my hands would start to freeze on the rungs. Finally, after what seemed like hours of climbing, I saw sunlight streaming in through a small door. Beyond the door my friends were waiting on the roof. I climbed over the top of the ladder and through the door. What a relief it was to be in the fresh air with something wide and solid under my feet.

"Watch out for the roof," Amos warned. "It's slippery."

Amos was right. Although not very steep, it was corrugated steel like the siding and not much to get a grip on even with sneakers.

Fats, Scuff, and Amos were sitting on a peak in the roof a few feet from the door. I sat down between Fats and Scuff. They both looked rather shaken. Fats was holding his head glaring down at the roof.

"I'm not going to set one foot on that ladder again," he grumbled turning to me. "You'll have to get a helicopter or something to get me down from here."

"Same with me," Scuff said.

I slapped Fats on the back and laughed. "If you hadn't gone up, I'd never climbed that stupid ladder."

"Humf!" he replied.

Weed finished the climb and came through the door onto the roof. "Nothing to it," he grinned.

"Nothing to it," Fats mocked under his breath. "Guess if you're stupid everything's fun."

"Let's scout around and see what the Truckers are up to," Mickey suggested, "but keep low and don't stick your head over the edge."

"Don't worry," Fats said, "I ain't moving one step on this roof."

"Me either," Scuff muttered.

"Okay, you two keep an eye on the ladder. Give us plenty of warning if you hear anything."

Mickey, Weed, Buzzy and Amos spread out over the roof. I stood on the peak. The building gave a terrific view of the railroad yard. I could see the old burlap mill down toward Sherwoods, the powdered milk factory off Route 23, all the creameries, feed mills, and coal lots, Snyder's Metal Works, the railroad station, the G.L.F. Farm Store, and most of the smaller barns, shops, and railroad sheds. I could even see the oil storage tanks next to the John Deere Garage on Elm Street.

"Hey, John, come here!" Amos called under his breath. He and Weed were crouched at the edge of the roof that faced the G.L.F. Farm Store. I dropped to the roof and shuffled crab-like over to where they were waiting.

"Look down, over toward the sheds," Weed whispered.

I carefully peered over the edge. About ten feet below was the narrow roof that overhung the loading docks, and below that a large feed truck. Standing by the truck, talking, were Bertie, Bones, and Turk. From somewhere near the back of the warehouse Jake called out. I couldn't see him but I saw Turk shake his head.

"They ain't got a clue," Weed chuckled.

"Yeah, they're never going to find us up here," I nodded.

Amos sat down and stretched out on the warm roof, making a pillow with his arms. "Yep," he added, "and sooner or later they're going to get bored and go home." He closed his eyes and within seconds had dozed off.

Somewhere in the distance I heard the low rumble of a diesel locomotive and followed the sound. A freight train was pulling out of the upper yard near the barrel factory, picking up speed as it approached the warehouse. Down the tracks a red pickup truck turned off the Walton Road and raced toward the G.L.F. Farm Store trying to beat the train. Weed saw the pickup too.

"Hey, that's the Johnsons from Hamden. I recognize the truck," he said. "Look, Melinda's in the back with her little brother. Get Buzzy!"

Buzzy was talking to Scuff and Fats. I took a penny out of my pocket and chucked it at him. It hit him in the back. When he turned around, Weed and I motioned him to come over.

"Me-lin-da," I spelled out with my mouth.

Buzzy jumped up, raced across the peak of the roof and stopped at the edge on our side.

"Look, Buz, it's your girl friend," Weed said, pointing at the pickup.

The noise woke Amos. He lifted his head and looked around. When he saw Buzzy standing at the edge of the roof he cried, "Get down! The Truckers'll see you!"

Buzzy didn't pay any attention. He'd seen Melinda in the pickup and was dancing about waving frantically.

"You idiot," Amos yelled and lunged forward to pull him down. But before he could get to him, Buzzy slipped on the corrugated metal, lost his balance, and fell over the edge. We watched in horror as he hit the narrow roof below and slid off. From there he fell almost two stories into the back of the feed truck hitting the pile of feed with a whump! and sending up a large cloud of dust.

The three Truckers standing near the truck began backing away. They didn't have the faintest idea what had fallen into the back of the truck. After a few seconds the pile moved and Buzzy crawled out. He was covered with feed. He stood up and began dusting off his shirt and pants. Bertie, Bones, and Turk looked on in amazement.

"Get him! Get him!" shouts burst from the rear of the warehouse. I looked back and saw Roy and Jake running full speed toward the truck.

Buzzy looked up and saw the three Truckers standing a few yards away. He leapt from the truck and took off running for the Walton Road. But Bones was already in motion. He tackled Buzzy around the waist and threw him to the ground. As the two boys wrestled in the dirt, Bertie and Turk started over. I knew Buzzy could handle Bones, but Bertie and Turk would have to be distracted. I stuck my fingers in my mouth and whistled so loud it made my ears ring. Turk and Bertie swung around and looked up at the roof. Roy and Jake stopped and looked up too. Weed saw what was up and yelled, "Hey, McGraw, I hear your mother wears army boots and eats slop with the hogs."

Turk's black eyes darkened. "I dare you to come down

here and say that, Shaw," he bellowed. "I'll tear you apart!"

Behind him Buzzy struggled to break away from Bones, but Bones wouldn't let go. Buzzy swung his fist over his shoulder and hit Bones square in the nose. Bones gave a yell and fell back dazed. Buzzy jumped to his feet and took off. Bones' yell alerted the other Truckers and they took off after him. Out across the tracks the boys ran. Buzzy headed for a string of boxcars, crawled under one of the cars, and came up on the other side. The Truckers had spread out in order to surround him. Beyond the boxcars the freight train from the upper yard was passing. Buzzy ran as fast as he could alongside the train, grabbed the ladder of a passing tank car and pulled himself up. Roy caught up to the car and tried to pull him off, but Buzzy kicked him away. The other Truckers were too far behind and had to give up the chase. Weed, Amos, and I cheered Buzzy's escape. Roy walked back to his friends. The five boys stood quietly for a moment watching us on the roof. Then Roy spoke to them and they headed back toward the warehouse. The remaining gang members had come from behind the building and were waiting by the truck.

Trapped

I heard a noise behind me and turned to see Mickey sliding down the roof towards us. He'd been on the other side and missed all the excitement. Fats and Scuff were hurrying over too.

"What's going on? Why are you guys yelling at the Truckers? Have you gone crazy?" Mickey shouted. "Now they know we're up on the roof!"

"Did something happen to Buzzy?" Scuff asked, ignoring Mickey.

"Yeah, he fell off the roof," Weed replied calmly.

161

"He fell off the roof?!" the three boys shrieked in unison.

"Yeah, he fell off the roof, but he's okay."

"Where is he now?" Fats asked.

"Probably on his way to Walton," I said.

"Walton?"

"Yeah, Walton."

Mickey looked bewildered. "You've got to explain what happened. First of all, how'd he fall?"

"He was waving to Melinda Johnson."

"Melinda who?"

"You know, Melinda Johnson from Hamden—in the ninth grade. Buzzy's has a big crush on her."

"Where was she?"

"In the back of her father's pickup truck heading for the G.L.F."

"And he slipped and fell four stories?"

"The loading dock roof broke his fall. He landed in a pile of feed in the back of a truck. Then he got chased by the Truckers. Bones caught him but he fought him off."

"How come he's on his way to Walton?" Scuff asked.

"He jumped the Walton freight."

Mickey, Fats, and Scuff gazed down the yard at the train as it rumbled out of the lower yard past the powdered milk factory.

"Now that the Truckers know we're up here," Amos said, "we'd better find another way off this roof—and fast!"

"We can jump down to the roof over the loading docks, then work our way around to the lower barn roofs," I said.

"Yeah, but once we jump down we can't get back up," Mickey warned.

Weed suddenly turned and faced the door. "I hear voices coming from inside," he said.

Amos hurried across the roof to the ladder. The rest of us followed. As we approached the door, Amos motioned us to stay back. Cautiously he stuck his head through the opening, peered down, and pulled his head back.

"Turk, Jake, and Bertie are down there. I think they've found the ladder."

"Where do you figure the rest of them are?" Scuff said.

"They must be looking for other way up," I replied.

"We got to get down from here," Fats moaned. "The Truckers are really mad. No telling what they'll do if they catch us up here."

"Probably hang us over the edge by our feet," Mickey said with a grim face.

"Probably throw us off," Weed laughed.

"That ain't funny, Weed," Scuff said.

Amos poked his head through the door again. "Jake and Turk are coming up!" he exclaimed. "They're on the ladder!"

We crowded around the opening. I could just see the tops of their heads in the dim light. Jake was ahead of Turk and about twenty feet up. Both of them looked nervous. Bertie was staying on the ground.

"Let's give them a thrill," Mickey said. He gripped one side of the ladder and began shaking it. Amos gripped the other side. The ladder rattled and swayed all up and down the wall. Jake and Turk let out a terrible yell and hugged the ladder with both arms. They looked pale as sheets.

"P-Please don't shake the ladder," Jake pleaded. "W-we'll leave you alone. We'll be friends. I promise! I swear!"

Mickey and Amos kept the ladder shaking. Slowly the two Truckers began inching their way back down. Once on the floor they let loose with a string of threats and curses that would have even amazed Shorty. Jake swore he'd throw Mickey and Amos off the roof head first if he got hold of them.

"Come on," I said, "they won't be coming up for a while. Let's find a way off this roof."

"The only way off this roof is to jump to the loading dock roof," Amos said.

"That's what I was afraid of," I sighed.

"Jeez," Fats groaned, "you guys are going to kill me yet."

The six of us got down on our hands and knees and crawled down the roof to the edge above the loading dock. Mickey positioned himself over one of the metal rods that angled out to support the dock roof and let his legs drop over the edge. Gripping the edge, he slowly slipped off. As soon as he hit the roof below, he grabbed the metal rod to keep from sliding off. It took my breath away just watching him. The roof was less than ten feet wide. Amos jumped next, then Weed and Scuff. When it came my turn I was shaking all over. It was an easier jump than to the boxcar, but I knew I'd tumble three stories if I missed the support. Only the thought of what would happen if the Truckers caught us up there kept me going. I dropped my legs over the edge and slowly eased myself forward. I wanted to close my eyes but feared I'd miss the support. Then suddenly I was flying through the air, hit the roof, and caught the support with both arms. I held on so tightly, I swung completely around it landing on my back.

"Kind of fun," I smiled as Mickey gave me a hand up. Inside I felt like I was going to lose what was left of my breakfast.

Fats was the last to come down. He had us all worried. We didn't know if he had enough strength to hold his weight, and there wasn't much room for us to help. Only Mickey stood by the support to try and grab him if he started to fall. As Fats eased himself over the edge, I found myself more scared than when I was sitting there.

"Geronimo," he cried weakly and down he came. As soon as he hit I knew he'd never be able to hold himself. He knew it too because he dove on his stomach. That saved him. He slid between the roof and metal support and groaned to a halt wedged between them. His arms and head were hanging over the edge. It was brilliant. Fats had more guts than all the rest of us put together. Mickey helped pull him out, and he joined us up against the building. Scuff and I gave him a big hug.

Keeping low, we began making our way single file toward the corner. Below I could hear occasional shouts from the Truckers. I was praying they wouldn't discover us. We were sitting ducks for rock throwing. Fortunately they were concentrating on the rear of the warehouse trying to find a way up. Only Bertie ran out in front along the dock, but he didn't look up.

Cautiously we rounded the corner to the west side of the building. There we came to a lower building with a flat roof. Attached to the building were numerous sheds. The dock roof ended a couple of feet before the flat roof. Amos ran along the dock roof and jumped to the flat roof. The rest of us quickly followed.

"Spread out and look for a way down," I said once we were all on the roof. "Keep an eye out for Truckers."

"Meet back here in a couple of minutes," Mickey added.

Weed and I headed for a long, two-story equipment shed at right angles to the buildings. Inside I could see trucks parked, and racks of tubing and lumber. We jumped to the roof and crawled along the peak looking for a trap door or ladder but didn't find either. When we got back all the others had returned except Amos. They looked pretty glum.

"Find a way down?" Mickey asked hopefully.

We both shook our heads.

"At least the Truckers haven't found a way up," Scuff muttered.

"Yeah, but what are we going to do if we can't find a way down?" Fats blinked.

"Maybe the fire department will have to come and get us down," Scuff suggested.

"The fire department!" Weed exclaimed. "We'll be the laughingstock of the town."

"Shhh, here comes Amos," Mickey interrupted.

Amos ran along a lower shed roof and vaulted up to the flat roof. "I found a way down!" he called under his breath.

We ran across the roof to meet him.

"Two sheds back there's a dead tree," he panted. "We can climb the limbs partway down, shimmy the rest. But we've got to be careful. Roy, Bull, and Bertie are just around the corner."

We started after Amos but only got a few steps when shouts burst out overhead. I looked up and saw Luke and Jake on the warehouse roof. Then Turk appeared. I figured Luke must have led the way up. Shaking the ladder would never have stopped him. We were lucky to have gotten off when we did.

The four boys pointed at us and yelled to their friends on the ground. We could hear shuffling in the gravel below but couldn't see what was going on. Then the top of a ladder banged against the edge of the roof.

"We got you now," Turk shouted. "You ain't going to get away this time."

As he spoke, Luke and Jake disappeared. I knew they were heading for the dock roof.

"Push the ladder off," I cried running for the edge.

Mickey, Amos and Weed were right with me. When we got there Roy and Bull had already started up.

"On three," I said, gripping the top. "Ready...one, two, three."

We pushed the ladder as hard as we could. Roy and Frank held on helplessly. It rose to the vertical, wobbled, and fell back against the building. The two of them quickly began backing down.

"Once more on three," I said. "One, two, three."

This time the ladder went right on over. The two boys leapt clear as it crashed to the ground. Roy immediately picked up a rock and sent it whizzing at us.

"Let's get out of here!" Mickey shouted.

Once again Amos took the lead and we followed. He ran to the end of the flat roof and dropped to a lower roof. The lower roof was L-shaped. The far end extended behind the warehouse. Just before I dropped down, I glanced back and saw Luke coming around the corner of the warehouse on the dock roof.

"Scutter's down," I shouted to others.

Amos led us to the far end behind the warehouse. In a narrow alley between the shed and the warehouse stood a dead locust tree with most of its branches broken off. One by one we leapt to the tree grabbing the stubby limbs. I was the last to come down. Luke and Jake were already on the shed roof and yelling to the Truckers below to get to the rear of the building. I leapt to the tree, shimmied partway down the trunk and dropped to the ground. My friends were waiting ready to run.

"The cable car—behind the station!" I shouted.

Race To The Cable Car

Off we raced across the barren strip of land that separated the warehouse from the train station. By the time the Truckers came around the side of the building we had a good fifty yard lead, but I knew we'd need every foot of it to get up to the cable car. We ran over numerous strings of tracks and past the station. An old man sitting outside the telegraph office leaned forward in his chair and waved to us. I managed a quick wave back. Ahead lay two more sets of tracks and an overgrown parking lot with a row of rusting truck trailers. Beyond the parking lot toward the river the cable car tower rose above a forest of bamboo and sumac.

As I approached the first set of tracks, a movement down the line caught my eye. Someone had been creeping low along the bed and was now running full out towards us. I felt a sudden panic. I was sure it was Gideon Spickey. But when I took a second look I was amazed to see that it was Buzzy. The others saw him too.

"Buzzy!" we all shouted excitedly.

"Head for the cable car," Mickey yelled motioning with his arm.

Buzzy cut across the second tracks and joined up with us in the parking lot. His pants and shirt were still dusty and he was running with a slight limp.

"Are you okay?" I asked.

"I twisted my ankle when I jumped the train, but it's okay," he replied.

"Thought you were in Walton," Weed said running up next to him.

"The train slowed at Sherwoods'. I jumped off. Came up the tracks. Watched you guys from the old turntable. I thought the Truckers had you on the roof."

"They almost did!" Fats puffed. "Never find the ladder Amos told us. What a joke."

169

"They only found it because Buzzy fell off," Amos protested.

"Cut the talk and run," Mickey yelled, "we've got to get to that tower."

I glanced back and saw that Mickey was right. Some of the Truckers had already passed the station and were gaining on us.

At the rear of the lot we pushed through the brush to a wire mesh fence covered with weeds and vines. The fence surrounded the cable tower. It stood above our heads but was bent down in places. We quickly climbed over and dropped into the thick grass on the other side. The tower stood about ten feet into the center. It was a two-story metal structure. The top supported a steel cable that extended out across the river to a cement block set in the steep bank on the other side. A ladder rose up the middle but ended at a deck with a padlocked trap door. Above the deck rested the cable car. It was used by the forestry service to measure the height of the river. I'd known about the cable car since I was a little kid, and sometimes borrowed it for fishing.

We hurried to the tower and began climbing the crisscross of struts and beams. Buzzy and I reached the top first. Carefully we worked our way out around the deck and swung up using the handrail. On top we found the cable car sitting next to the cable. It was a shallow wooden box with two overhead pulleys attached to a metal frame. We picked it up and set the pulleys on the cable. There was only room for three of us in the box. The rest would have to hang on.

As we moved to the rail to give the others a hand, I saw that Roy, Gideon, and Bones had already scaled the fence and were almost to the base of the tower.

"Come on!" I yelled, "they're at the tower!"

Quickly the others swung up to the deck. Fats and Amos were last. As Amos rolled over the handrail, Gideon scurried up the tower so fast he came within inches of grabbing his foot.

The seven of us piled into the car as best we could. Arms and legs stuck out everywhere. Weed and Mickey were hanging on the back and gave a shove off the deck. The car coasted out over the brush and trees but groaned to a halt at the edge of the river. It was badly overloaded. Luke, Jake, and Turk had run to the bank and were waiting. They began packing balls of river mud and slinging them at us. We were sitting ducks.

"Got twenty-five cents in my pocket for anyone knocks one of them off." I heard Turk say.

But we had worse problems than getting pasted with mud balls. Having gotten on the tower deck, Gideon, Roy, and Bones had climbed out on the cable and were moving hand over hand towards us. If they got to the car we'd all end up on the ground.

"Pull on the cable!" I shouted.

Unfortunately only Buzzy, Mickey and I had our hands free. The others were either clinging to the sides or squashed in the bottom. The three of us gripped the cable and pulled as hard as we could. The pulleys creaked and slowly the car coasted out over the river. But after a few yards it ground to a halt. The barrage of mud balls intensified. One glob hit me so hard in the neck that I bumped heads with Fats.

"Keep pulling!" Mickey yelled.

Once again the three of us pulled as hard as we could. This time the car built up enough speed to coast almost to the middle of the river. That gave us a good lead on the Truckers hanging from the cable but it didn't stop them. From the middle to the concrete block on the bank we had to pull all the way. When we finally reached the bank my arms felt like they were going to fall off. Buzzy, Mickey and I could hardly pull ourselves out of the car.

171

We dropped to the ground and lay there exhausted. I could feel clots of mud in my hair and down my back.

"They're crazy!" Scuff exclaimed.

"Sure are," Amos and Weed agreed.

I lifted my head and saw that the three Truckers were still coming after us on the cable. They were approaching mid-river. It was worse than being chased by mad dogs.

"Let them come," Weed said, "we can handle the three of them."

"Yeah, Weed, we'll let you take on Roy all by yourself," Fats scoffed.

"I've got an idea," I said getting up. "Quick, find some big rocks and put them in the car."

We spread out along the slope gathering rocks and brought them back to the car. "That's enough," I said when the bottom of the wooden box was covered. "Everyone in back now and we'll send her off on three."

I waited till everyone was in position and began slowly counting. "One...two..." With each count we rocked the car back then forward, and on three sent it humming down the cable. The three

Truckers watched in horror as it raced toward them. Gideon was in the lead. He held on until it was inches away hoping it would stop—but it didn't. One by one the boys dropped into the river. We burst into howls of laughter. The car continued along the cable and finally came to a stop a few yards from the tower. The boys swam back to shore where they were helped out by their friends. For a few seconds the Trucker gang stood silently on the bank glaring across the river at us. Then they turned and walked back toward the railroad yard.

"Wheeew!" Buzzy cried, falling into the grass.

Amos shook his head and gave a little whistle. "What a day," he sighed. "If we've got nine lives like a cat, I'll bet we used at least eight today."

"Think they might be planning to cross the river and sneak up on us?" Fats wondered.

"Not a chance," Mickey said. "They'd have to swim or take the Kingston Street bridges. Turk and Bull can hardly swim, so that leaves the bridges. It would take them a half-hour to get here."

"Anyone want an apple?" Amos asked.

"Yeah!" we replied enthusiastically.

"There's an orchard up in back of here. I'll get some."

Amos climbed up the steep bank and disappeared over the top. He soon returned with his shirt bulging with bright red apples. He tossed a couple to each of us. We lay in the soft grass for a long time munching apples and listening to the birds and crickets along the bank. In the distance the west branch of the Delaware River flowed out across the flats. Beyond the flats rose green wooded mountains, and beyond the mountains great billowy clouds filled the sky.

"Ever wonder what's beyond those mountains?" Buzzy gave me a nudge.

I nodded.

"We should raft down the river someday."

"Yeah," I agreed, "maybe early summer—when the water's still high."

"Yeah," Buzzy smiled, "raft right on down to the ocean."

Big Sister And Wally Tibbs

After supper, Buzzy, Weed, Mickey, and Scuff stopped by the house on their way to the movies at the Abbot Theater. It was a double feature: Gene Autry in "Apache Country" and the Bowery Boys in "Private Eyes." I told them I didn't feel like going. Besides trying to save money for a new fishing pole, I was tired from our afternoon of getting chased all over the railroad yard. We argued for a while and they finally left without me. I kicked off my sneakers and sat down on the front steps. The evening air was cool, but the stone steps were still warm. Puffles, our big gray Angora cat, jumped up from chipmunk hunting in the pachysandra to join me. I sat for a long time watching the occasional cars go by and exchanging greetings with neighbors strolling the sidewalk. Puffles finally got bored and chased off after a cat prowling the Lackland shrubs. At about seven-thirty Wally Tibbs pulled up in front of the house in his red convertible Ford coupe. He climbed over the windshield to the hood and with one deft leap slid across the hood and landed upright on the sidewalk. It was a neat trick.

"Save it for my sister," I yelled to him.

He gave a bow and started up the walk. His blond hair was carefully slicked down, clothes fresh out of the Oneonta Prep Shop, and shoes the latest black and white bucks. I watched him, wondering how long before he'd become ancient history in my fickle sister's date book. She had guys calling her all the time.

174

"What you up to tonight?" he asked approaching the steps. "Busting streetlights, stealing cars, slinging apples at old ladies?" He gave a big laugh.

I laughed too and shook my head. "Nothing exciting, just hanging around."

He stopped at the steps, reached into his pants pocket and pulled out a quarter which he flipped to me. I caught it and looked at him wondering what he wanted.

"Keep me informed about the competition—know what I mean? I heard Buddy Herman's been dogging around."

He gave a nod and I nodded back. I liked Wally in spite of his slick hair and showy duds. His parents owned a fuel oil business. He was an only child and a bit pampered but good-natured and always friendly to me. Around school he wasn't much into sports but instead worked on the student newspaper and yearbook, starred in all his class plays, and played clarinet in the band.

Up the steps Wally hurried and gave a long ring on the bell. In his hand he now held three violets which he'd taken from inside his jacket. Shortly Kaye popped out. "Ohhh!" she sighed seeing the flowers, took them, and carefully placed them in her hair behind her ear. They gave her dark blue eyes an almost violet appearance. The two of them skipped down the steps holding hands and raced for the car. Wally gallantly threw open the car door and Kaye dropped into the red leather seats.

"Stay out of mischief, little brother," she sang out as Wally shut the door.

Stay out of mischief, little brother! She was less than a year older than me. We'd been practically raised twins. Now suddenly she's fourteen, in high school and going out on dates, and I'm some sort of goofy little brother.

As I grumbled under my breath, Wally jumped to the hood and prepared to make the same deft leap he'd made before. Unfortunately he failed to see Miss Farley Heatherington, the town librarian, coming by the car on her three-speed English bike. I yelled a warning, but it was too late. Off the hood he sailed, right over Miss Heatherington's front wheel. The two collided head to chest with a sound flat rocks make when dropped into mud. Miss Heatherington bounced backwards, slid off the seat, and landed in a heap on the pavement. Wally remained straddling the bicycle, dazed but upright. Slowly Miss Heatherington sat up. She replaced her faded straw hat and adjusted the steel-rimmed glasses that hung from one ear. Giving an audible groan, she rose from the street and dusted herself off. She was a big, solid woman, about fifty, with a stern countenance and quick temper. Sufficiently dusted, she turned to the bicycle. Wally was terribly flustered and babbling all sorts of apologies. He jumped to the side and held the bike as if it were a prize steed. Miss Heatherington gave him a brief furious glance and jerked it away with both hands. She stepped over the crossbar, engaged the pedal and pushed off down the street. Wally pulled a neatly folded handkerchief from his shirt pocket and wiped his brow.

"You two should get together and do a circus act," I called, trying to ease his embarrassment.

He smiled and squeaked out a tight little laugh.

"Bet that's the most excitement she's had in years," I continued. "She'll probably dream about you for weeks."

He waved me off and climbed into his car. After making sure Miss Heatherington had turned off at the library path, he started the car and cautiously drove up the street.

"Stay out of mischief, big sister," I stood and yelled after them.

Amanda James

The coupe turned onto Kingston Street and disappeared over the bridges. I sat back down and leaned against the front door. Elm Street remained deserted for a long time. The sun settled into the mountains, and a scattering of stars appeared overhead. Inside the house I could hear a flurry of violins from my mother's classical music program. Sometimes she sang with the music. She had a great soprano voice. I usually enjoyed listening to the music, but tonight I was thinking about other things. I was thinking about the girl with the antique baby carriage. I'd thought about her all through supper. She was really nice. She had come over and sat down right next to me when I was fixing the wheel. I wondered if she liked me. My friends thought she did—except maybe for Weed and Scuff. I wondered if I should go up and visit her. That's what I'd wanted to do all evening. But maybe she was just being polite about the wheel, and she'd be upset if I stopped by her aunt's house uninvited. I'd feel terrible if she told me to go away. She probably had a boyfriend somewhere anyway. But she seemed pleased when I told her I lived in town; and she told me where she was staying—even described her aunt's house. She wouldn't have told me all that if she didn't think I might stop and visit her. It was as good as an invitation. But maybe she, Kate, and Jeanne had planned a party this evening with Fritz, Joe, and Tony. She'd be having lots of fun and would have forgotten all about me. I'd knock at the door and they'd all stare at me wondering what I was doing there. I'd feel like an idiot. Jeez, I didn't even know her name.

It was a real predicament. I got up three times and started across the lawn, but stopped and moped back to the steps. The neighbors must have thought I was crazy. Then Miss Heatherington pedaled back down the street from the library, and that gave me a great idea. I'd bicycle down Sheldon Drive like I was coming from the school, casually coast into the Crawford driveway at the bottom of the hill and see if maybe the girl was on the porch or around the yard. That way I could always say I was heading home and just stopped to say hi. It was brilliant. The only problem was getting up to the school without passing the Crawford house. I'd have to take a round-about route.

I ran to the barn, jumped on my bike, and raced out across the lawn for Sherwoods. It was dusk now, but there was still plenty of light to see the road. I made Sherwoods Bridge in record time. A few hundred feet beyond the bridge I cut onto an old dirt logging road and pedaled hard up to Route 28. At Route 28 I headed back toward town. Soon Delaware Academy and Central School came into view, and a steep road split off to the right. I took the steep road which ended at the bus drop-off near the front of the school. Up over the lawn I pedaled and around the side of the building to the play-ground area. A group of boys were talking outside the chain-link fence surrounding the blacktop basketball courts. Two were sitting on bicycles. It was too dark to make out who they were but one of the bicyclers looked like Luke Scutter. I continued through the rear parking lot and was approaching the stone wall entrance onto Sheldon Drive when I heard two bicycles coming up fast behind me. There were shouts, and I recognized the voices of Luke Scutter and Gideon Spickey. I hit the pedal so hard the front of my bike almost lifted off the road. Through the entrance I tore and full out down Sheldon Drive, but Luke and Gideon were faster. By mid-hill they were only a few feet off my rear wheel and moving up on either side.

"We're going to get you, Hoffie," Luke cackled.

"We want to see if you can fly," Gideon laughed.

I was so scared I thought my heart was going to explode in my chest. My only chance for escape was to suddenly brake and hope they shot by. As we hit maximum speed approaching the foot of the hill, I slammed the breaks so hard I felt the metal pedal guard cut into my sneaker. The coaster brake screamed and the rear tire ripped against the rough pavement, but Luke and Gideon weren't fooled. As Gideon went by he belted me in the ribs. Then Luke caught me by the shirt and almost dragged me off the seat. I spun around backward out of control and crashed to the pavement. Fortunately the end of the handle bar hit first and broke my fall. The bike bounced a few yards and finally slid to a stop in the loose gravel. I was still clutching the handlebars. As I lay in the road wondering if I'd broken any bones, I heard someone run up.

"Are you okay?" a concerned voice cried.

I looked up and saw a girl dressed in tan Bermuda shorts, a plaid blouse, and sandals standing at the edge of the road leaning toward me. I recognized her as the girl with the antique baby carriage.

"Are you having a party or something?" I asked still somewhat dazed.

She looked puzzled. "Do you need an ambulance?"

"No," I said slowly standing up. "I guess I'm okay."

"Oh! It's you—the wheel fixer!" she exclaimed and hurried over.

I nodded and picked up my bike. It was a wreck. The handlebars were all twisted, the rear wheel was bent and one pedal hung loose.

"It's pretty bad," she noted.

"Yeah, I'm going to need more than a pair of pliers to fix this," I sighed.

"Why didn't your two friends stop?" she asked.

"They weren't exactly friends. They're members of a gang up on Meredith Street."

"Were they after you?"

"Yeah," I nodded, "they knocked me off my bike."

"They knocked you off your bike! Are you going to call the police?"

"Gosh, no!" I said somewhat surprised.

"Why not?"

"Well...I couldn't do that. Police have other things to do—like catching speeders and bank robbers."

Her green eyes darkened and her face grew serious. "It's foolish not to tell the police, really foolish! You could have gotten hurt."

I hung my head and shrugged. It wasn't half as foolish as bicycling all the way to Sherwoods, up a logging road to Route 28, back to town, and around the school just to get to the foot of Sheldon Drive—a three minute walk by the Kingston Street bridges.

For a few seconds I could feel her staring at me. I didn't know what to say or do so I pretended to be fiddling with

180

the bicycle. Then she stepped over next to me and said, "Come on over to the porch. I'm babysitting my cousin. I'll get some ice cream and ginger ale. We'll make sodas."

"Yeah," I said, "I'd really like a soda."

She started for the house but stopped after a couple of steps and turned back. "My name's Amanda," she said. "What's yours?"

"John," I replied.

"John," she repeated slowly, turned and ran across the lawn for the porch. She ran so gracefully her sandals hardly seemed to touch the grass. I watched until she disappeared into the house. Then I picked up my battered bicycle, wheeled it up the driveway and rested it against a tree by the porch. As I started up the porch steps, Amanda came out the front door carrying a tray of spoons, glasses, ice cream, ginger ale, and potato chips. I hurried to help her, and we set the tray on a small table. After making sodas, we both sat on the porch swing and looked out across the sparkling lights of the town.

Amanda took a deep breath and said, "It's so quiet and smells so good here. In the city there's always the smell of car and bus fumes, and sirens and horns are always blowing."

"You live in the city?" I said.

"New York City," she nodded.

"Do you have a house?"

"No, we live in an apartment. It's right off Central Park. I can see the park from my bedroom window. Mom and I go walking there every Sunday after church. Then we treat ourselves to croissants. Sometimes in the afternoons we go to a play or a musical or maybe even an opera. Sundays are always fun."

"What's a cross-ant?"

"A croissant. It's just a fancy roll," she smiled.

"Do you eat a lot of fancy foods? I heard that city people eat a lot of fancy foods."

"We have baked potatoes every Monday and spaghetti on Thursdays. That's not so fancy."

"No, that's not fancy at all."

We sat quietly for a few seconds.

"Do you go to school in the city?"

"A private school. It's only a couple blocks from home. Dad got an apartment so I wouldn't have to take the bus."

"What's a private school?"

"You have to pay to go there—like when you go to college; and they get to teach whatever they want."

"Why don't you go to a regular school?"

"Because my parents wanted me to go to a special school."

"What's special about your school?"

She laughed, tucked her legs up under her and looked very thoughtful.

"My school is very special—and it's different. I have friends in other private schools, and they tell me my school is really different. First, I've had the same teacher, Mr. Whitman, since first grade. He's called my class teacher. Each class in my school has its own class teacher from first to eighth grade."

"Wow, the same teacher since first grade! Don't you get kind of tired of him?"

She shook her head. "Next to Mom and Dad, Mr. Whitman's my favorite person. But I didn't always like him. Sixth grade was pretty awful. He was always picking on me, and I was always arguing. I even wanted to leave the school. I wanted to go to Mrs. Hadley Parker's School For Young Actresses, but my parents wouldn't let me. Seventh grade was great. Mr. Whitman really changed. Next year I'll be in eighth grade."

"What else is special?"

"We have main lesson first thing every morning. It lasts from eight-thirty to ten-thirty. Then we have a break."

"Main lesson?"

"Umm," she nodded sipping her soda, "we study a subject for three or maybe four weeks—like poetry or geography or art, then we get a new subject. They're called blocks. History blocks and plays are my favorites. This coming year our class is putting on Romeo and Juliet. It's going to be lots of fun. Math and science blocks are the worst. Unfortunately you have to take all the blocks; you can't skip any. We don't use any text-books either. Mr. Whitman teaches us everything him-self. We write essays and draw pictures and make our own books for each block. It's kind of fun, but it's hard work too. I've got all my main lesson books since first grade in my closet. Sometimes my friends come over on rainy days and we compare our books and remember all the silly things we did when we were little kids."

She stopped talking for a moment and gazed at me with a curious look. I'd never met anyone who talked as fast as Amanda, but she was sure fun to watch. Each time she spoke her short wavy hair bounced with the words and her hands painted pictures in the air. And when she smiled her one dimple showed.

"Oh!" she sat straight up. "I forgot to mention eu-rythmy. Twice a week we do eurythmy." She lowered her voice to a monotone. "The human body as an instrument for speech and music. Behold ..."With her arms spread wide she arched them into a circle in front of her and her finger tips just touched. "Oooo," she spoke letting the sound slowly fade. She next quickly crossed her arms in front of her and said "A". Then her hands shot forward and made a little dive. "Ffff," she spoke.

She sat up straight again. "That was speech eurythmy. Pretty neat?"

I was a bit confused but nodded.

"Now I'll show you tone Eurythmy."

She stretched her arms out to either side of her and hummed a series of notes. With each new note she carefully raised or lowered her arms.

"See," she said, "it's easy—but of course we're moving on our feet at the same time. It's like dance. The boys have to do it too. They complain a lot, but that's because they're so clumsy and fool around."

I figured I'd be clumsy and fool around too trying to do all that stuff with my arms and legs.

Amanda twirled the ice cream in her soda with her spoon. "Do you like school?" she asked.

"It's okay," I shrugged. "Gym and recess are fun. I daydream a lot in class. This past year Kurt Hadlock, a big farm kid, sat right in front of me. I kind of scrunched down behind him, rested my head in my hands and dozed away."

"Do you play an instrument?"

I gave a big sigh. "Yeah, violin. Tweets Laney and I are the only boy violinists in the whole junior orchestra. Most of the time I just try to keep my bow going in the right direction. I've been playing for two years and still can't read a note of music. Mom won't let me quit."

Amanda sighed too. "I play viola. I've been playing since third grade."

"I'd really like to learn guitar," I said. "I picked up an old busted Gibson guitar at an auction. Glued it back together. Trouble is, the nearest teacher's in Oneonta, and lessons cost three dollars. That's a week of lawn mowing money."

As I finished speaking a car approached the driveway. Amanda turned and got up from the swing.

"It's my aunt and uncle. They're back from shopping. I'll introduce you to them."

"It's kind of late. I'd better get going," I said jumping up. "Maybe some other time."

I hurried down the porch steps and picked up my bicycle.

"Can I see you tomorrow?" I called back.

She shook her head. "I'm leaving in the morning. I'm taking the early bus to New York."

"Are you going to visit again?"

"Maybe in October. Kate and her friends are having a Halloween party."

The Crawford car pulled up to the house. Amanda waved, and I waved back. Then I ducked into the shadows of a row of maple trees. Boy, I thought to myself as I headed down the hill to the bridges, Amanda sure is nice—and pretty too. I wish she lived in Delhi. I'd go up and have sodas with her every night.